**Welcome to the www.blinddatebrides.com member profile of:**
**Sanfrandani (aka Danica Bennett)**

### My ideal partner…

Probably doesn't exist outside the covers of my Jane Austen collection. I'm independent. I don't want a guy to be the center of my world, and I'm not sure I want to be any part of his. Getting my career back on track is my number one priority.

### My details…

- **Age:** twenty-six

- **I live:** in San Francisco

- **Marital status:** single

- **Occupation:** sales (don't ask)

### You'll match if you…

- Are between twenty-four and thirty-five

- Don't leave your heart here

- Are single and want to stay that way

- Are employed

Read the rest of Sanfrandani's profile *here*
**www.blinddatebrides.com**

**Private IM chat between Kangagirl, Sanfrandani and Englishcrumpet:**

**Kangagirl:**
*What were you thinking? This profile doesn't sound anything like the Dani we know and love.*

**Sanfrandani:**
*That's okay. I'm not exactly surfing for dates.*

**Englishcrumpet:**
*But we found our Mr. Rights. It's your turn now.*

**Sanfrandani:**
*I'm not looking for Mr. Right.*

**Kangagirl:**
*But he may be looking for you!*

**Englishcrumpet:**
*We can help you modify your profile.*

**Kangagirl:**
*Yes! A few changes and you'll have more dates than you know what to do with.*

**Sanfrandani:**
*Thanks so much, but there isn't a lot of room in my life for dating. My new job isn't exactly what I thought it would be, and that's... complicating things. But I found you two here, so joining blinddatebrides.com has been worth every penny!*

# MELISSA McCLONE

## *Dream Date with the Millionaire*

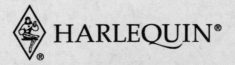

TORONTO • NEW YORK • LONDON
AMSTERDAM • PARIS • SYDNEY • HAMBURG
STOCKHOLM • ATHENS • TOKYO • MILAN • MADRID
PRAGUE • WARSAW • BUDAPEST • AUCKLAND

Recycling programs for this product may not exist in your area.

ISBN-13: 978-0-373-18448-4

DREAM DATE WITH THE MILLIONAIRE

First North American Publication 2009.

Copyright © 2009 by Melissa Martinez McClone.

www.eHarlequin.com

**Printed in U.S.A.**

Introducing a brand-new, exciting trilogy
from Harlequin Romance®!

*From first date to wedding date!*

Meet three very different women from around the world,
and follow their stories as they find friendship,
love and their happily ever afters with a little help
from the world of online dating!

**April 2009**
*Nine-to-Five Bride* **by Jennie Adams**
Meet Kangagirl from Sydney, Australia,
aka Marissa Warren.
She's turning thirty and is looking for
Mr. Nice and Ordinary!

**May 2009**
*Blind-Date Baby* **by Fiona Harper**
Meet Englishcrumpet from London, England,
aka Grace Marlowe.
Her teenage daughter has left home, and
Grace is looking for a second chance at love!

**June 2009**
*Dream Date with the Millionaire*
**by Melissa McClone**
Meet Sanfrandani from San Francisco, U.S.A.,
aka Dani Bennett.
She's a career girl who doesn't have time for love—
or so she thinks!

**Three women, three countries,
three exciting love stories.
Watch it all unfold @ www.blinddatebrides.com.**

To Jennie Adams and Fiona Harper,
my blinddatebrides.com cohorts
and new chat buddies

Special thanks to:
Markus Frind with plentyoffish.com,
Virginia Kantra and Gary Yngve

# CHAPTER ONE

Blinddatebrides.com is running thirteen chat rooms, fifty-six private IM conferences, and 7828 members are online. Chat with your dating prospects now!

Private IM conference #25 (3 participants)…

Englishcrumpet: Who would have thought I'd meet the man of my dreams at an online dating site? I still can't believe it!

DANICA BENNETT blew out a puff of air. She couldn't believe it either.

Alone in her neatly organized cubicle in the otherwise cluttered and messy San Francisco office of Hookamate.com, she reread the purple words written in a funky font on her computer screen. Englishcrumpet, aka Grace Marlowe from London, deserved to be happy. Dani sincerely hoped her friend would find happiness and wedded bliss with her new husband, Noah. Especially with a baby on the way.

But Dani wasn't so sure living happily ever after was possible. She glanced at the photograph of her family—her mother, her three younger sisters and herself. Winning the lottery seemed more likely. Though she'd never say those words to her newly wed friend. Dani typed, the letters appearing in green—the color of money. Too bad her life couldn't be as rich and bold as her computer font.

Sanfrandani: It is pretty amazing.

Grace had only known Noah a short time before marrying the bestselling thriller author and then found out she was pregnant.

More words, rust-brown in a plain but strong font, appeared on screen. Kangagirl, their friend Marissa Warren, from Australia.

Kangagirl: Amazing, yes, but not that rare. Apparently one in eight people meet their spouses online.

Dani almost laughed. Marissa sounded like a commercial for online dating. Or like a happy bride. Which she would be in a few months. She'd fallen in love with her temporary boss, not someone she met on Blinddatebrides.com like Grace. Though it wasn't for Marissa's lack of trying to meet a guy online.

Sanfrandani: Well, it's a good thing for me. Or I'd be out of another job.

Even this crappy job, she thought to herself and stabbed her fork at her lunch, a limp chicken Caesar salad leftover from last night's dinner.

Englishcrumpet: What do you mean?
Kangagirl: You've lost me.

The two messages popped up on Dani's screen at almost the same moment.

Oh, no. She dropped her fork. Distracted by her friends' happiness and her own bleak prospects, she'd revealed more than she intended. The three of them had grown so close over the past six months she'd almost let her secret slip out.

Time for damage control.

Sanfrandani: Nothing. I'm just so glad you guys joined Blinddatebrides.com. I don't know how I would have survived these months without your support and friendship.

But typing the words gave Dani a funny feeling in her stomach. What kind of friend was she? Keeping the truth about what she was doing at Blinddatebrides.com from Marissa and Grace.

Englishcrumpet: You've been through a lot, Dani. Losing your dream job and getting used to your new one. Things will turn around. Just watch.
Kangagirl: And then, when you least expect it, you're going to meet him. That one special man.

Dani hoped not.

Snores drifted from the engineers' cubicle a few feet away. Someone must have pulled an all-nighter.

She needed to get her career back on track first. She'd spent the last six months trying to find another job with no success. Distractions, especially men, weren't allowed right now.

Kangagirl: The only question is…how do we make it happen?

*We.* Unexpected tears stung Dani's eyes. She ran her fingertips over the bracelet—silver with crystal beads—Marissa had sent her after a trip to Hong Kong. These women, even though they'd never met in person, truly cared about her.

Sanfrandani: Please. No one needs to make anything happen. I'm doing fine. No worries.
Englishcrumpet: We're not really worrying. We just want to help. You joined this site for a reason, Dani.

But not the same reason as Marissa and Grace.
Guilt welled up inside Dani.

It was time to come clean. To stop lying.

Her fingers flew across the keyboard with light-ning speed, in case nerves and fear got the best of her. Or her boss showed up.

Sanfrandani: I didn't join Blinddatebrides.com
to meet men.
Kangagirl: Then why did you join?
Sanfrandani: Because

The cursor blinked, waiting for her to finish. Dani swallowed hard. Her online friendship with Marissa and Grace was the only thing in her life going well these days. Did she want to risk that?

But what kind of relationship did they have, really, if she couldn't be honest?

Dani took a deep breath and typed.

Sanfrandani: I was forced to.

She stared at the screen, her heart racing, her hands sweating.

Englishcrumpet: Did someone sign you up like
my daughter did with me?

Oh, dear. Dani snuck another look around the office before returning her trembling hands to the keyboard.

Sanfrandani: No, I signed up myself.
Kangagirl: ???

Dani felt sick, but the truth had to be said. Er, typed.

Sanfrandani: I'm a spy.

"There's something you should see."

Bryce Delaney heard his assistant's voice, but didn't glance up from his computer monitor and the database query he was writing. He didn't have to.

Joelle Chang would be standing two feet from the edge of his walnut-stained desk holding a manila file folder with a pen—blue ink only so she could tell the difference on photocopies—tucked behind her ear. Despite her college-girl long hair and trendy clothes, forty-one-year-old Joelle was dedicated, thorough and one-hundred-percent predictable. Exactly the way he liked things. And people. "I pay you enough to see for me."

"You said you wanted to be kept in the loop about possible security issues."

Security. A top priority at his Web site Blinddate-brides.com. Bryce looked up. "Possible or probable?"

Joelle's almond-shaped eyes grew dark. "Two red flags."

Damn. He didn't need this on top of the other problems they'd been dealing with. Scammers, spammers, hackers, marrieds, the list went on.

"It might not mean anything," she added.

In the last year, there had been a handful of false alarms. "But it could mean we have a trouble-maker on board."

It wouldn't be the first time. He'd dealt with escorts, cheats, thieves and liars. Had charges brought against them when possible, too.

Bryce wasn't about to let anyone take advantage of his customers. Too many people pretended to be something they weren't, both in real life and online. He had experience with that. His sister, too. But she was more trusting than him. That was why he'd started a dating—make that a relationship—Web site: to protect good people like Caitlin.

"What do you have?" he asked.

Joelle handed him a file. "This particular client has been a member of the site for over six months. Everything about her looks good, including her background check."

"Her?"

"Yes," Joelle answered. "None of the e-mail filters have picked up anything to suggest she's an escort."

Those were usually easy to detect since they asked for money in almost every e-mail.

"But the chat filter picked up something so we did a little investigating," Joelle said. "The subject spends hours logged on to the site each day, but she has not accepted a date yet, even though her profile has been marked highly compatible with several men."

Bryce had worked with a psychologist to create an algorithm to match clients based on their interests, backgrounds and personalities. Chats, based on compatibility, were also arranged with groups of well-matched people, too, since many people preferred group interactions to one-on-one. Some clients, though, preferred to peruse the profiles themselves and pick matches that way.

He opened the file and studied the photo of a woman. The messy blond hair piled on top of her head and secured with a—was that a red bandana?—caught his eye first. Not the most appealing hairstyle. The picture itself was far from flattering. She wasn't smiling or looking at the camera. Shadows obscured what he could see of her face, though she looked flushed unless her skin was always red like that. Her profile stated blue eyes, but he couldn't distinguish the color, really anything about her. "She's been matched?"

"Yes. The compatibility program has matched her with seventeen clients so far. Five of those contacted her. Others must have seen something they liked in her profile because they e-mailed her, too. She replied back to each one, but that was it. No additional correspondence. No chat invites. Nothing."

"At least she's following the guidelines about replying to others even if you're not interested in them."

"Yes."

He read more in the file. Turning down potential dates wasn't unusual. Bryce remembered one shy female client in particular, but others in the past had misrepresented themselves. Better to err on the side of caution. "You've taken the usual steps?"

Joelle nodded. "Customer service called to discuss her experience so far. She asked as many questions as they did, and they were on the phone for two hours."

"Two hours?"

Another nod. "I called her myself after that. She came across as highly intelligent and very friendly, but remember that identity thief? Never assume anyone who is nice is also harmless."

"That's for sure." Bryce flipped through the pages in the file. He noticed a familiar zip code. She lived here in San Francisco. Many of the scammers he'd dealt with lived overseas. But this was on his home turf. He could follow the prosecution to the end if she were guilty. "Where does she go on the site?"

"Chat rooms, particularly the Ladies Lounge, and

private IM conferences. She spends most of her time exploring the Web site. Not client profiles, but the content itself."

Most people, whether they wanted to date or not, liked checking out the profiles of people in their area. On some Internet relationship sites that earned revenue through advertising; anyone could register and search profiles for free. Not on Blinddate-brides.com. Only paying members, who'd filled out a detailed questionnaire and agreed to a background check if they lived in the United States, were allowed to search the database, read profiles and contact members.

Joelle continued. "She's online during normal work hours as well as late at night. Two different IP addresses have been linked to her account name, depending on the time of day."

Nothing unusual about that. "Work and home."

"Seems likely, but I don't know many employers who would encourage their employees to spend that much time each day at a dating site while at work."

"Unless the boss doesn't know." Bryce skimmed the rest of the pages and saw one of the red flags. She'd said she was a spy during a chat. "Or she has an employer who wants her checking us out."

The online dating world was cutthroat. The competition stole from each other regularly, but pretending to want to meet dates went against the terms of service users agreed to when they joined Blinddate-brides.com. But she hadn't mentioned anything about her job prior to her saying she was a spy.

"What does she do for a living?" Bryce asked.

"She listed sales as her occupation," Joelle said.

"That's too vague, given the list of options she could have chosen."

"Red flag number three?" Joelle asked.

Bryce nodded. He prided himself on making his Web site a safe and secure place to meet and fall in love. His sister had had her heart broken, as well as her bank account drained, thanks to the "love" she'd found on a competitor's site. The guy had turned out to be the exact opposite of what he'd claimed to be. No one was going to pull a stunt like that on Bryce's site, during his watch. "I'll get right on it."

Joelle smiled. "I almost feel sorry for her."

"Why is that?" he asked.

"Because, once you get started, you don't stop."

He shrugged. "Just doing my job."

"Remember, it's just a job." She pulled the pen from behind her ear. "Grant is e-mailing you a file with additional information you might need."

"Thanks." As she left the office and closed the door behind her, Bryce stared at the picture in the folder. He glanced at the user name. "Who are you, Sanfrandani? And what are you doing on my site?"

* * *

At three o'clock, Dani sat at the rectangular table that functioned as the "conference room" as well as the "break room" with her five coworkers at the fledgling Internet dating site Hookamate.com. Pacing back and forth across the floor of the converted warehouse was their boss, James Richardson.

James wore ripped-at-the-knee jeans and a black T-shirt. He had long, straggly blond hair. He spoke fast and loud, as if fueled by caffeine and junk food. He reminded her of a stereotypical computer science graduate student in desperate need of a balanced meal, sunshine and a girlfriend, but his first two Internet ventures had made him tons of money. He'd sold them, and now wanted to replicate that success with a new online dating site.

Succeed at any cost, Dani had finally figured out.

During her interview, James had seemed more captivated with her double-D bra cup sized breasts than the qualifications on her résumé. Yet he'd surprised her by asking detailed questions about her schooling and work experience. He'd known exactly what he wanted in a marketing person.

She had the skills so she'd made the most of what nature had given her, just as her mother had taught her to do, and secured the job. Which meant she only had herself to blame for where she found herself today. She wanted to bang her head on the table for her stupidity.

"The good news is we had an increase in traffic thanks to Danica's marketing efforts." James winked at her. No one at the company except him knew she was undercover, so to speak, spying on the local competition, Blinddatebrides.com. "Unfortunately the traffic exceeded our capacity so we've been having to add machines. But that's not a bad problem. Traffic will drive our advertising revenue. That means more money for us. Anyone have other ideas to generate more users?"

No one said anything.

"Rethinking our branding might help," she suggested. "Taglines, image, ads, name."

James clenched his jaw. "Our Web site name rocks."

"Totally."

"Yeah."

Dani listened to the men in the room support their boss who they held in almost cult leader esteem. The only other woman at the table, Shelley, the office manager, shook her head and mouthed the word *sorry* to Dani.

The responses didn't deter her. She had to do something. Say something.

"Look at Blinddatebrides.com." The name of the fastest-growing competitor brought groans from the three engineers at the table, but Dani kept going.

"When people hear Blinddatebrides.com, they can't help but think about brides. That word connotes weddings, which makes people think relationships, marriage, permanence. That's appealing to users."

"Only if you want to end up with a ball and chain," a Ruby on Rails developer named Andrew murmured.

Dani ignored him. "Granted, your…I mean our…site's name does have 'mate', but 'hook' makes people think of…"

"What?" James asked.

"One-night stands," a PHP programmer, who probably hadn't showered let alone had a date in a month, said.

People—okay, guys—laughed.

"Yeah, sex," the interface hacker offered. "Sex appeals to a lot of people, too."

The two men gave each other high fives.

Dani sighed. "I worry the name brings about images of hookups, not serious relationships."

No one spoke.

"There's such a thing as a niche market," Andrew said. "Hookups can be our niche."

She stared at all the nodding heads. Male heads. No wonder women had a hard time finding good men to date these days. Not that she was interested in anything to do with dating.

"I appreciate you bringing this up, Danica," James said finally. "I'll have to think about what you said."

Which meant he would never mention it again. That was how things worked around here. James's way or the highway. He'd given her a choice—join Blinddatebrides.com or quit. She needed the paycheck so did as he'd requested. Up until that point, she'd really liked the challenges of being in on the ground floor of a start-up again. Now she hated getting up in the morning.

"Anything else?" he asked.

No one said a word. No one ever did. Except her. She didn't know why she bothered.

"Get to work, people." James clapped his hands together. "We don't want anyone to be lonely tonight. They need to hook a mate!"

Dani trudged back to her cubicle, frustrated and tired. She'd stayed up late last night sending out another batch of résumés. Speaking of which, she'd better check her e-mail in case someone had replied. She clicked on her in-box. There, at the top, was a new message, but not from a potential employer. This was one was from bigbrother@blinddatebrides.com with the subject header "I read your profile."

Oh, no. She squeezed her eyes shut. Another guy who wanted to get to know her.

Her stomach churned. She hated this. Sure, she could just hit "delete"—that was par for the course on many dating sites—but Blinddatebrides.com was different. The site touted itself as a community where politeness and manners mattered. Users were requested to reply, even if the intent was to give someone a brush-off. Still, the thought of telling another guy she wasn't interested in getting to know him better made her feel physically ill.

But what else could she do?

Leading a guy on when she was on the site under false pretenses ranked right up there with corporate spying in her book. She massaged her forehead to stop a full-on headache from erupting. Okay, one rejection wasn't going to send some guy scampering back to his mommy in tears, but…

Why did this keep happening?

Dani had taken steps to ensure it wouldn't. What sense of honor she had left had made her fill out the profile questionnaire truthfully so she understood when the compatibility program deemed her a match with someone. But Dani had hedged against the computer algorithms by uploading the most unattractive photo of herself she could find. She looked downright ugly. While other women uploaded more than one picture to their profile page, she hadn't.

She'd also downplayed her interests to make herself sound…well…about as exciting as a slug inching across a driveway at dawn. She'd listed the library as her favorite place to spend a Saturday night and a collection of Jane Austen novels as her must-have item if stranded on a desert island.

No man should want to date her.

Maybe this one didn't. Maybe he was one of those guys, the players, who only wanted to have sex. If that were the case, she wouldn't mind telling him to get lost.

Dani opened her eyes and read the entire e-mail.

To: "Sanfrandani" <sanfrandani@blinddate-brides.com>
From: "Bigbrother" <bigbrother@blinddate-brides.com>
Subject: I read your profile
Who are you searching for? Mr. Darcy? Or Mr. Knightley?
-bb

Dani reread the message. Twice.

Okay, she was impressed this guy knew the names of two Jane Austen heroes, but who did he take her for? Intelligent, impulsive Lizzy or smug, interfering Emma?

Still, his message intrigued Dani. She typed a reply and hit "send." With a satisfied smile on her face, she leaned back in her chair. And almost fell over backward.

Uh-oh. What had she done?

She shouldn't have replied. Dani grimaced. She wasn't supposed to engage Bigbrother in more e-mails. She was supposed to tell him she wasn't interested. To. Go. Away. Politely, of course.

Only she hadn't wanted to do that.

Not when his e-mail had been unlike any of the others she'd received. He'd obviously read her profile and asked his question based on what she'd written. Not on her photo or bra size. Maybe he was genuinely interested.

Or maybe he was ugly.

Her eyes locked on the link to his profile that would transport her to a page all about him, a page with his picture.

Curiosity trickled down the length of her arm to her fingertip, hovering above the laptop's trackpad. She wanted to know more about Bigbrother. Read what he'd written about himself. See what he looked like.

Temptation flared. She moved the cursor to the link. All she had to do was click, but she couldn't.

The less Dani knew about Bigbrother, the better.

She wasn't looking to meet a guy. She didn't want to meet a guy. Especially one from Blinddatebrides.com.

Not under these circumstances.

Ignoring the twinge of regret, she closed his e-mail. Goodbye, Bigbrother.

# CHAPTER TWO

As Bryce sipped his coffee, hoping the caffeine would get him through the rest of the day, he stared at the four hundred unread e-mails in his in-box. No way could he get through all of them in the next fifteen minutes, but there was one reply he hoped to find.

He skimmed the list of senders and found the name he was looking for...

Sanfrandani.

That didn't take long.

He couldn't curb his suspicions and wanted to see what she had to say. Which would it be? A polite brush-off or a straight-to-the-point-please-don't-contact-me-again? Curious, he opened the message.

To: "Bigbrother" <bigbrother@blinddate-brides.com>
From: "Sanfrandani" <sanfrandani@blinddate-brides.com>

Subject: RE: I read your profile
Desperately seeking...Colonel Brandon.
-sfd

Bryce frowned and reread the e-mail. He called Joelle into his office. "Who is Colonel Brandon?"

"Didn't he kill Miss Scarlet in the library with the—"

"No. That's a game. This one is in a book. Jane Austen."

Joelle stared blankly at him.

"Come on," he said. "You have to know this."

She raised a finely arched brow. "Because I'm female?"

"Because..." Oh, hell, she had him there. "Yeah."

"I majored in Economics, not English Lit."

Bryce had majored in Computer Science. He pressed his lips together, still staring at the screen. "Wasn't there a movie?"

"Not that I saw. Not with a Colonel Brandon. Colin Firth, now... Yum."

"Spare me."

Joelle shrugged. "Guess you'll have to Google this Colonel guy, then. Or call your sister."

Caitlin.

Thinking of his younger sister brought a smile to Bryce's face. Of course, Caitlin would know the answer. She was a font of movie trivia, especially chick flicks, but a call to her would lead to a lengthy discussion about wedding preparations. Bryce was happy she'd found the love she'd been hoping for on Blinddatebrides.com. Keeping her safe had been his main reason for creating the Web site, but he didn't have time to discuss whether champagne-pink or midnight-blue would be the better choice for bridesmaids' dresses. And he didn't want her probing him about whether he'd found a date for her upcoming engagement party yet.

His search query resulted in 336,000 documents. The Colonel was a character in Jane Austen's *Sense and Sensibility*, but the descriptions Bryce read didn't make sense. One article called the Colonel "sad and reserved." Another said he was a "dull older man."

Nothing, however, explained why Sanfrandani was desperately seeking the Colonel. She was twenty-six, according to her profile—too young for such an old, boring guy. Unless she was a gold-digger.

Bryce stared at Sanfrandani's picture. Even though he couldn't make out any of her facial features, she seemed to have a graceful neck. And that red bandana was starting to grow on him. Still, a woman after a rich husband would have uploaded a better photograph.

But why had she responded to him so mysteriously, almost playfully, instead of telling him to get lost? She'd brushed off the other guys who had contacted her. Was she leading Bryce on? Or not?

He was annoyed. Intrigued.

Attracted.

Not attracted, he corrected. This was an investigation, not a flirtation.

Bryce needed more information so he could figure out where she was coming from and what kind of game she was playing. Then he would know what to do. As he hit "reply", he heard a commotion outside.

He hastily typed a response. He would have rather taken his time, but that wasn't an option right now.

"Look at this," someone yelled outside his office. "Am I really seeing this?"

A low hum buzzed.

Not a good kind of noise either.

Bryce hit "send" with a twinge of regret, but he needed to find out what was going on out there.

"SQL injection."

The words stopped him cold.

"No way."

"It can't be."

He understood the disbelief in the voices. The denial.

"It is."

Damn. Bryce bolted to the door. Someone had entered an executable code disguised as data into the site. No doubt trying to steal credit card and other personal information from the database.

Outside his office, the noise level increased exponentially, his team springing into action like an Emergency Room staff with multiple casualties coming in. Except these injuries weren't as easily diagnosed, and the damage unknown.

"Run forensics on the logs," Bryce ordered.

"Already on it," Christopher, a rock-star caliber software engineer, said.

Bryce nodded his approval. "We need a snapshot of the database right now."

"I'll do it," someone said from across the room.

"Let's patch the hole, people. Compromised data?" he asked Grant, his number two employee.

Compromised data—the stealing or copying of customers' personal information—would be a PR nightmare. Even if credit card account numbers hadn't been captured, there was the issue of privacy. Online dating may have become an accepted way to find love, but some people would be embarrassed to have their anonymous use of the Web site become public knowledge.

Grant rubbed his hand over his face. "We don't know yet."

"Okay." Bryce projected calm. "Then let's find out."

He wanted to jump into the trenches and dig his fingers in. Bryce was a techie at heart, but he was also the boss. Sometimes the two didn't mesh well together. Today he would make sure things worked. He couldn't afford for them not to.

"Should we shut down the site?" Grant asked.

Bryce shook his head. "Not unless we have to."

"Don't want to lose the revenue?"

The money didn't matter to Bryce right now. This was personal. "I don't want to tip off the hackers. Not if we can nail them."

"It's a mess in here," someone murmured from a few desks away.

Bryce imagined himself as one of the Jane Austen heroes Sanfrandani liked to read about, ready to clean up the mess and save the day. Yeah, right.

He sat at an empty desk, one being set up for a new hire, and logged on to the system to double-check the database. Bryce wanted to see that personal information—everything from names and passwords to credit card numbers—was encrypted. The data was. "How strong is the encryption?"

"Strong enough to keep a 100,000-computer botnet busy for years," a security specialist answered.

Good news. But Bryce was still going to have to call their lawyer as soon as he had a better handle on things. It was going to be a long day. And most likely an even longer night.

* * *

Talk about a long day.

Dani stretched her arms above her head. She needed a nap but would settle for more caffeine. She'd spent her afternoon working on search engine optimization aka SEO. Increasing traffic to the site was a big part of her marketing job. The more hits, the more clicks. And that meant more money—advertising revenue. But turning visitors into repeat users was important, too, and sometimes harder to do. Especially when the site lacked the type of content it needed to draw people back. Content she'd found on Blinddatebrides.com. Content she now had to create for Hookamate.com.

Too bad she was more interested in checking her e-mail every five minutes to see if Bigbrother had replied. She'd never been like this before, waiting for some strange guy to e-mail her, disappointed when he hadn't.

Pathetic.

That was what she was.

And distracted ever since she'd checked out Bigbrother's profile. Talk about making a big mistake with a single click.

He lived in San Francisco and was cute in a geeky sort of way. In his picture, he wore a San Francisco Giants baseball cap pulled low on his brow. Dark hair stuck out from the sides. He was dressed casually in a Boston Red Sox shirt and a pair of faded jeans. The photo wasn't a close-up, but she caught a hint of a smile on his face. He almost looked…shy. She liked that.

A beep sounded. Dani checked her e-mail again. Jackpot.

Bigbrother had replied. Anticipation unleashed the butterflies in her stomach. She couldn't wait to see what he'd written. She opened the message.

To: "Sanfrandani" <sanfrandani@blinddate-brides.com>
From: "Bigbrother" <bigbrother@blinddate-brides.com>
Subject: Colonel Brandon
You're searching for a dull old guy who wears a uniform?

The oh-so-romantic-loves-unconditionally Colonel was near perfect in her mind, but she could see how some might see him as a dull old guy. Especially a man who, based on his attire in his profile picture, preferred baseball to Jane Austen. Dani laughed.

"Care to share the joke?" James asked.

She turned in her chair. Her boss stood at the entrance to her cubicle.

Her cheeks warmed, but then she realized she had nothing to be embarrassed about. James was the one who wanted her checking out the site. "It's an e-mail from someone on Blinddatebrides.com."

James's eyes narrowed. "A male someone?"

She nodded. "Just doing my job."

"A good job at that." He beamed. "So when are you going out with him?"

"I'm not," Dani said with a twinge of regret. Bigbrother was the only one of the men who had contacted her that she wanted to meet.

"Too many other fish to fry?"

Oh, boy. He had that all wrong. "Uh…no."

"So he must be a loser, then. How many other guys have you met from bdb?" James never called their local competitor by their full name. He seemed to have it in for them, but she didn't know why and was too afraid to ask.

"None," she admitted.

He gave her the once-over. "It can't be from a lack of offers. None of them meet your standards?"

"Nothing like that." She peered over the cubicle walls to see if anyone was around or listening. "I can't accept any dates," she whispered.

"Why not?" he asked. "And why are you whispering?"

"Because of the…you know."

"I don't know."

She lowered her voice more. "The spying."

James sighed. "It's called market research,

Danica. Every company does it, so please get over your aversion to your job responsibilities."

Checking out a competitor was one thing, but market research had never made her feel so tacky or dirty, as if she were doing something she wouldn't want her mother to know about. In fact she hadn't told her mother about it. Or her sisters. The only people who knew besides James were Marissa and Grace. Dani wanted to keep it that way.

"I need to know everything about bdb," he continued. "That includes their clients."

The expectant look in his eyes sent a shiver down her spine. "You're not suggesting I—"

"Go out with them," he said at the same time. "Meet whoever contacts you. Dates are the perfect opportunity to check out whether bdb customer expectations are being met or not. You can put together a profile of their users for me, too."

Her shoulders slumped.

When James had told her she would have to get her hands dirty with all facets of Internet marketing she had no idea this was what he meant.

"I can't do this," she said. "I won't lead guys on."

James grinned. "They won't mind. Any guy would be thrilled to date a woman like you. Trust me."

Her boss was the last person she trusted, but she knew what he meant. Most men never saw past her curves to her personality. Or even the color of her eyes. But this felt… "It's still wrong."

"What's the big deal, Danica?" James sounded irritated, as if she'd told him the Web site needed to be patched again to work on Internet Explorer 6. "Meet them for coffee. Cupcakes. Conversation. You don't have to sleep with them unless you want to."

Dani's stomach roiled. "This is a—"

"Start with the guy who made you laugh," he interrupted.

Excitement shot through her. Okay, she liked the idea of meeting Bigbrother, especially with her boss giving her permission, but that wouldn't be fair. "I really don't think—"

"It's not your call." James read the e-mail on her screen. "Bigbrother, huh? I wonder what's big about him."

She cringed. The guy did not look like a player. Far from it. She was worried she might hurt him.

"Hit 'reply'," James ordered.

Dani didn't. She couldn't.

A part of her wanted to quit. Right now. But, with her student loans and family obligations, she couldn't afford to be without a decent paycheck. That was the one thing she had to say about her boss—he paid well.

James reached around and hit "reply". "Tell him you want to meet him for coffee."

"But I don't want to meet him for coffee. I have no idea who he is. I know absolutely nothing about him."

Nothing except he intrigued her. The way he'd approached her. His brief e-mail. His quick reply. His picture.

"If you don't ask him out," James said with a steely glint in his eyes, "I will."

Dani gulped. She knew he would follow through on the threat. "I'll do it myself."

James didn't move. A muscle flicked at his jaw.

"I can reply right now," she added.

Dani started typing an invite to coffee, aware and annoyed that James was peering over her shoulder.

"Make sure you tell him the meeting is your treat," he said. "That can make a difference to some guys."

Darn James anyway. Her exchanges with Bigbrother had been fun and flirty, but her boss was ruining it. "Do I get to expense it?"

James tossed a twenty on her desk. "No expense form needed."

Dani hit the "send" button, lobbing the ball back over the net to Bigbrother's side of the court. The next move was up to him. She was torn over how she wanted him to respond. She hoped he ignored her request or said no because she didn't want to mislead him, but a part—a large part—wanted him to agree to meet her.

Just then another e-mail from Blinddatebrides.com appeared in her in-box. Maybe she'd lucked out and the system had kicked her reply for some reason. And then she saw the sender's name. Gymguy. Oh, no. Not another one. She shook her head.

"Woo-hoo," James said. "Looks like you're Miss Popular. Want some help replying to Gymguy?"

Dani sighed. "I know what to do."

Unfortunately.

"Thanks, Danica," James said, backing out of the cubicle, much to her relief. "I won't forget all that you're doing for the site."

She stared at the twenty. Neither would she.

"How's it going?" Joelle entered Bryce's office carrying a pizza box with a paper bag sitting on top.

The scents of oregano and freshly baked crust made his stomach growl. He glanced at the clock. Eight o'clock? He'd lost track of time, but wasn't surprised with everything going on.

"Trying to stay a step ahead of the scammers isn't easy. They may have found a hole, but they couldn't crack the encrypted format." That unfortunately wouldn't stop them from trying to steal information again. Every time Bryce's engineers changed some-thing, the hackers would modify their programs to try and get around the new security. It didn't help matters that they used stolen credit cards to register and pay for membership. If only he could run background checks on everyone who wanted to join, not just U.S. citizens. That would crack down on foreign scammers. "Talk about a cat and mouse game. It's never ending."

"Just remember to eat," Joelle said.

"The team—"

"I ordered enough food for everyone."

Always thinking. Always one step ahead. Sometimes Bryce thought Joelle could read his mind. "Thanks."

She opened the bag and pulled out a Styrofoam box and packets of Parmesan cheese and chili peppers. "Start with the salad, please."

He grabbed a slice of sausage and mushroom pizza from the box and bit into it. "You're sounding a lot like my mother."

"You think?" Joelle's mouth quirked. "Well, then, as soon as you fix this problem, why don't you reward yourself by seeing if those matchmaking algorithms you developed can find you a few dates?"

An image of Sanfrandani with her red bandana around her head popped into his mind. Bryce nearly choked. He swallowed and wiped his mouth with the napkin. "You've been talking to my mother. Those words are straight out of her playbook."

Joelle's cheeks reddened. After six months of his mother's lectures about his dating more, he'd finally told her no more. She'd stopped. Now he knew why. She was trying to have Joelle take up the cause.

"You have a profile set up," Joelle said. "You should keep it public all the time, not just when you're investigating clients or trying to flush out scammers."

"I'll tell you what I told my mother," Bryce explained. "I spend all my time working on Blinddatebrides.com. It's a win-win situation. Others find love. I make a whole bunch of money. I can't handle a relationship of my own right now."

He thought about his e-mail exchange with Sanfrandani. That was the closest he'd come to flirting in…weeks. Or was it months?

"Can't or won't?" Joelle challenged.

"You know I can fire you."

She tilted her chin. "Yes, but you'd never be able to replace me."

True. One of the most successful online dating Web sites was a one-man show, but Bryce needed help. Joelle handled everything from finances to human resources. She didn't mind answering the phones, either. Her title of Business Manager was far too bland for all she did. Business Goddess would be a more apt description. He couldn't run Blinddatebrides.com without her. He knew it, and so did she. "Are you this hard on Connor?"

"Harder," she admitted. "But my husband knew what he was getting into when he married me. You, however, had no idea when you hired me."

"No regrets." Bryce winked. "At least none yet."

She smiled. "You have to admit, it would be excellent PR if you married someone you met at your own site. Just look at the interest in your sister's engagement."

"Stop. Now."

"Okay. I'll stop. Only because I know you have more important things to do right now, but tomorrow—"

"Out."

"I'm going." With a grin, Joelle walked out of his office.

As Bryce waited to hear from one of the engineers, he ate dinner. He'd forgotten everything that didn't involve the SQL injection, but now he couldn't stop thinking about one thing. One person really. Sanfrandani. Had she replied yet? He hoped so.

Checking his in-box, Bryce found a message from her. The corners of his mouth curved. The thrill of the catch, he told himself, and opened the e-mail.

To: "Bigbrother" <bigbrother@blinddate-brides.com>
From: "Sanfrandani" <sanfrandani@blinddate-brides.com>

Subject: RE: Colonel Brandon
Wrong on all counts except the uniform.
Could go either way there. The Colonel was
always there for Marianne. That's what makes
him a true hero.
But I won't hold it against you if you meet me
for coffee tomorrow morning. Eight o'clock.
Crossroads on Delancey. My treat.
-sfd

So she was…assertive. Interesting. And she'd
picked a great place to meet—a café that hired
people who had hit rock bottom and were trying to
turn their lives around. But he was wary.

Why would she make a date with him when she'd
rejected everyone else?

It obviously wasn't his knowledge of Austen. He
looked again at the screen. *Wrong on all counts.*

So…was Sanfrandani a spy? A scammer? Worse?

He pulled up her profile on the Web site and ran
a compatibility match with his questionnaire. The
program deemed them highly compatible, possible
soul mates. That surprised him.

He stared at her picture. The lighting was a
little better than on the print version he had, but
not by much.

Bryce didn't like being caught off guard, but it
had happened more than once today. Flushing out

the scammers who probably used hacked computers to do their dirty work with the SQL injection was
near impossible, but catching Sanfrandani might
actually be…fun.

What did she want?

Only one way to find out.

*Coffee tomorrow morning. My treat.*

Bryce smiled. He was looking forward to it.

Remember, Dani. Proposals made after one
cup of coffee are rare. Have fun!

Marissa's instant message delivered while Dani
had slept brought a needed smile to her face. She'd
been a bundle of nerves ever since Bigbrother
accepted her invitation to coffee.

Stop thinking about that. Him.

Don't think of the meeting as a date. Consider
it market research.

Grace's instant message echoed what James had
said. Good advice Dani intended to follow. She
wasn't going to let Bigbrother's profile picture or information blind her to her purpose. Okay, so she'd
really liked what he'd written about the importance
of family. But she knew from experience most guys
would say anything to get what they wanted. Big-

brother was probably misrepresenting himself at least a little.

She winced. And she was misrepresenting herself a lot.

Face it, getting to know Bigbrother wasn't possible under these circumstances. Thinking about him as anything other than market research would be a mistake. Downright wrong. He was not a potential date. He couldn't be.

And neither could she be one for him.

Dani liked what she'd seen about Bigbrother. He looked like a nice guy, the type who might be a little shy and easily hurt.

She would not be responsible for leading him on.

Time to scare him off.

She walked into her closet.

Fortunately, most guys never looked past the surface. All she had to do was keep the packaging relatively unattractive and her breasts covered, and he'd lose interest.

Her hand wavered over the fitted jeans and sharp jackets hanging on the rod and settled instead on an ex-boyfriend's pair of sweats and an oversized hoodie from her college days. She braided her blond hair into a single plait and tied a bandana around her head. She didn't put on any makeup, but stuck on a pair of sunglasses.

She squinted at the results in the full-length mirror hanging on the back of the closet door. Perfect.

Perfectly awful. She grimaced.

Dani took the bus to an area locally referred to as SoMa, south of Market, filled with loft warehouses, galleries and restaurants. As she walked toward South Beach and the café, a place known for giving second chances—something she desperately wanted herself—her breath hung on the air. Mornings in San Francisco were usually cold and foggy, no matter what the time of year.

As she stepped inside the café, warm air blasted her. The scent of freshly brewed coffee and pastries filled the loftlike open space and made her mouth water. A good thing. She planned on spending every cent of James's money this morning.

Hearing the din of the other customers, Dani glanced around. She'd stared at Bigbrother's picture enough last night she should be able to recognize him, but none of the people sitting on the couches and chairs looked familiar. Maybe she'd beat him here. Or maybe her darkened sunglasses kept her from seeing clearly. She moved toward an empty table.

"Sanfrandani?" a male voice asked.

Dani turned. A man, sitting at a table back against the wall near the bookstore portion of the café, was staring at her. She took a closer look, resisting the urge to push her sunglasses up above her forehead.

Thick dark lashes framed clear, warm eyes. Brown, maybe black, hair carelessly styled, as if he'd run his fingers through it, not a comb, fell past his collar in the back. His hair hadn't looked like this in his picture or maybe the cap had hid it. Either way, his hair changed his looks completely. But she wasn't complaining. In fact, Dani wouldn't mind running her fingers through his hair. "Big... brother?"

He nodded.

Heaven help her. The contrast between his dark hair and lighter complexion and eyes was, in a word, stunning. Talk about a picture not doing someone justice. His photo made him look cute, but didn't show his true appearance at all.

Was he hiding something, like her?

Dani was willing to take that chance.

As she walked toward him, he stood. Wowsa. He was tall, over six feet. Fit, trim, perfect. Men who looked like him only existed in magazines or the movies or her dreams. Yet she was having coffee with him. Her pulse quickened.

*Pull yourself together.*

Dani extended her arm. His large warm hand engulfed hers, his shake solid. She cleared her throat. "Nice to meet you."

He pulled a chair out for her. Good manners. "Thanks for suggesting this."

She wanted to thank his parents for having him and James for forcing her to ask Bigbrother out. Intelligent, handsome, polite. A blind date couldn't get much better than this. Or him.

Dani took the seat he offered. "You're welcome."

He sat across from her. Their gazes met.

Her heart bumped.

Oh, boy. She crossed her legs, tilted her head and gave him her best buy-me-a-drink smile.

He looked faintly startled.

Why…?

"I'm sorry I didn't recognize you." She leaned forward just a little.

"It's an old photo," he admitted. "Good thing I had no trouble recognizing you from your picture."

Dani frowned. "My…"

And then she realized. That picture. No wonder he looked taken aback.

Bigbrother was totally hot.

And she looked totally…not.

# CHAPTER THREE

BRYCE watched Sanfrandani tug surreptitiously on the waistband of her baggy sweats and bit back a smile. Nice hips. But the clothes… She looked like a kid who'd dressed with her eyes closed or a coed slumming in her boyfriend's clothes.

Obviously she didn't care what kind of impression she made on him.

He could find her confidence attractive.

Or insulting.

"What will you have?" she asked, standing in line to order.

"Two shots Americano."

She pushed her sunglasses on top of her head to read the menu. "Breakfast?"

"No, thanks."

She turned her head. "Sure?"

He stared into her sparkling blue eyes and suddenly wasn't sure about anything. Where had those beauties come from? "I'm not hungry."

She stepped up to the counter to order. "A two shot Americano, a white mocha and one lemon-poppy seed waffle."

Bryce pulled out his wallet as the barista, a young man with pierced ears and a tattoo on his forearm, pulled the shots.

Sanfrandani handed the bright-eyed girl behind the counter a twenty. "My treat, remember."

Confident, he thought again. And it was attractive.

"You pay," he said. "I'll carry."

A beat passed. And another. "Fine with me."

As she put her change into her wallet, Bryce gave her the once-over. Okay, all was not lost. He could see raw material there, hidden under the bulky sweats. With those pretty baby blues and full lips most women would pay big bucks to have, Sanfrandani wasn't so bad.

She raised an eyebrow. "See something you like after all?"

Bryce broke into a reluctant grin. "I'll stick to coffee."

"Suit yourself."

He picked up their drinks from the counter, followed her past a leather couch to their table against the wall.

Sitting across from him, she took a sip of her white mocha and licked foam off her upper lip. "Just what I needed."

A strand of blond hair had fallen out of her braid and threatened to slip into her drink. Without thinking, he reached forward and tucked it behind her ear. Her hair was smooth, her cheek warm.

She narrowed her eyes at him.

Bryce sat back, feeling foolish. "Your hair…it was about to fall into your whipped cream."

"Oh." She flushed. "The curse of long hair, I guess."

"Is that why you wear the bandana?" he asked.

She touched the cloth, as if to remind herself she was still wearing it. The simple gesture reminded him of Caitlin, when she was little and wore a tiara every day.

"I thought you might be some kind of cowgirl or something."

"Ha-ha. Actually…" she leaned her elbows on the table, cradling her drink in both hands "…I used to work in a stable."

Bryce studied her oval nails with their pretty pink polish. She didn't work in a stable now. "Tell me about it."

"It's not that exciting." She smiled and took another sip from her mug. "My mother works on a farm in central California. I mucked stables there and at a couple of ranches to earn money. I used bandanas to keep my hair out of the way. They also work well as sweat rags and, if you wet them, neck coolers when it's hot outside."

His family had horses—Caitlin wanted to start riding competitively again. He knew what the work involved and was impressed. "That's a hard way to earn money."

"Yes, but it was worth it. Not only did I get stronger cleaning stalls, but I got to exercise the horses when their owners couldn't." The words almost tumbled from her mouth with excitement. Her face became animated, but she seemed to catch herself and calm down. She raised her cup. "So now you know where my attachment to bandanas comes from."

"A worthy attachment, I'd say." His respect for her grew. He recalled her picture. The shadows. Her red face. Something clicked for him. "The photograph in your profile. Was it taken while you worked at one of the stables?"

She nodded. "I still help out at the farm when I visit my mom. One of my sisters took the picture with her cell phone as a joke."

Definitely a horse-lover. No one else would offer to help out with that job. But that didn't explain her using the unflattering picture.

"Why did you use that photo on your profile?" he asked.

She hesitated. "I wanted to make sure men were more interested in who I was as a person rather than my appearance."

"That makes sense." So maybe she was on the up-and-up. Caitlin had done the same with her profile picture. "Have you found any guys who passed the test?"

"You're here."

In spite of his suspicions, he liked her. "I am."

A café employee placed a plate and syrup in front of her. "One lemon-poppy waffle."

Bryce liked that she wasn't one of those women who lived off salads, rice cakes, nuts and seeds in order to stay a size zero. He also liked her self-confidence. "I'm glad I'm here."

She spread butter on the waffle. "The bandana didn't scare you off."

"It would take more than a bandana to scare me," he admitted. "Do you wear it every day?"

"No." She poured syrup on her waffle. "But bandanas come in real handy on those days I'm rushing out the door."

"Were you rushing this morning?"

She stared down her nose at him. "What do you think?"

That no woman would go to such lengths to look less attractive than she really was. "You were either in a rush or prefer comfort over…"

"Style," she offered.

He smiled. "You said it, not me."

The tension seemed to evaporate from around her

mouth. "I do like to be comfortable, but I may have taken being comfy to the extreme this morning. Next time I'll take a little more time getting ready."

"Next time, huh?" He watched her take a bite of the waffle. A drop of syrup hung on the corner of her lips. Damn, she had a sexy mouth. "So do you do this a lot?"

She wiped the syrup off with a napkin. "Go out for coffee and have breakfast?"

"Online dating."

"Oh, no." She stared at her plate, then raised her gaze to his. "You're my… This is my first time."

Bryce looked for a sign she might be lying. But she was making eye contact. Her voice pitch hadn't changed. She wasn't fidgeting or blinking. Then again, she might just be a good actress.

He picked up his coffee. "What do you think?"

"Well, so far so good," she said. "The mocha is delicious, the food tasty. Ask me again when we're finished, and I'll tell you how the company was."

Bryce might not trust her, but she was bright and had a sense of humor. He was enjoying this. Her. He sure hoped Sanfrandani wasn't guilty of anything. "I will."

"What about you?" she asked. "Do you rush getting ready in the morning or take your time?"

He sipped his drink. Strong and hot, the way he liked his coffee. "I'm a guy. Once we're out of high school, it's pretty much shower and go."

"Mm." She looked him over, taking her time but keeping her opinion to herself. "Well, at least no one could accuse you of being metro."

"Thank you." The amusement in her eyes brought a smile to his face. "I think."

"So I'm a newbie at this online dating thing. What about you?" she asked. "Have you gone on a lot of dates with people you met through Blinddate-brides.com?"

"Not a lot, much to the chagrin of my mother and sister."

"Why is that?" she asked.

"Both of them think it's time I settle down."

Dani raised her mug. "Do you think it's time to settle down?"

"No." Bryce found her easy to talk to. Strange, considering his reasons for wanting to meet her. "But my opinion doesn't matter much where my mother is concerned. She has been lecturing me about being over thirty and single. She wants grandchildren to spoil. My sister, who is a member of the site, has jumped on my mother's bandwagon and sends me links to the profiles of women she thinks I should contact."

"Your younger sister, right?"

"Yeah. How did you know?"

"Your user name is Bigbrother."

He nodded. "Caitlin picked the name for me."

"That's so sweet."

"She's a sweet girl. Woman," he corrected. "Sometimes I forget she's all grown up."

"And how does she feel about that?"

"She thinks I'm overprotective. Overbearing and a bully, too."

Sanfrandani's smile lit up her face. "The two of you are close."

It wasn't a question. "Yeah, but Caitlin drove me crazy when we were kids. Following me everywhere. I wanted to trade her in for a brother, but I couldn't help but watch out for her back then, too."

"That sounds so familiar. I watched out for my three little sisters, even though there were days I wanted to kill them. But I knew if I did that it would destroy my mother so I controlled myself."

He grinned. "I'm sure three younger sisters were much worse than one."

"Especially trying to get ready for school with only one bathroom for the four of us."

"Catfights?"

"Every day." She laughed. "How about with your sister?"

"She's one of my best friends, even though I still watch out for her."

"Lucky girl."

"She might disagree about that." Though Caitlin's

luck had changed for the better. Contentment settled in the center of Bryce's chest. "She recently got engaged to a man she met on Blinddatebrides.com."

"That's exciting news."

"Very." He smiled, thinking about Caitlin, all bubbly and glowing, showing off her diamond engagement ring. She'd thanked him for creating the Web site where she'd met her fiancé. That moment had made all his work, the sleepless nights and constant fires needing dousing, worth it. "My sister and her fiancé prove the matchmaking algorithm works, since that's how they found each other."

Sanfrandani set her fork on the plate. "You believe the algorithm actually works?"

He understood the doubt in her voice. Turning matters of the heart over to a machine wasn't easy. "I do. Relying on the program is the easiest and smartest way to find a compatible date."

"It's difficult for me to accept a computer could do a better job picking a date for me than I could."

"Is that why you haven't gone out with anyone before?" he asked.

"It didn't seem right."

Her response set off warning bells in Bryce's head. "Right?"

"The right time," she clarified. "But the compatibility program did work for a friend of mine who lives in London. They are married and expecting a baby."

"I'll have to tell my sister. She wants everyone to be as happy as she is."

"I have two friends like that. The one with the baby on the way and another who is engaged. I met both on the Web site," Sanfrandani said. "They're always pushing me to go out more. They mean well, but the…"

"Pressure."

"Exactly." She drank her coffee, seeming completely at ease. "Luckily, my mother doesn't care if I get married or not."

"She's not on the grandma track, then."

"Not at all. The only thing she wants is for me and my three sisters to pursue our passions and follow our dreams, whatever they may be."

Bryce wondered what her dreams entailed. "She sounds like a great mom."

"My mom's the best. My hero." Sanfrandani's eyes softened, as did the tone of her voice. "She raised us on her own. We didn't always have a place to sleep at night, but we always had food to eat and we knew we were loved. No matter what was going on, there was always more than enough love."

Her words squeezed Bryce's heart. No place to sleep sounded like she'd been homeless at times. No one should have to go through that, especially an innocent child. Maybe her background explained the way she acted and her ambivalence about dressing nice for their date.

He thought about his silver spoon upbringing— the overabundance of toys and clothes, the mansion and vacation homes, the revolving door of stepparents and the trust fund he'd never touched. His parents loved him, but they were so busy with their own lives and marriages, they'd often left him and Caitlin in the care of nannies. He couldn't say more than enough love existed at his house. Houses. "Sounds like you still had everything you needed in spite of the tough times."

"I didn't think so then, but growing up like that made me stronger, more determined."

"To do what?"

"Succeed. Make it on my own. Show the world I'm more than what they think I am." She raised her chin, then looked down. "Sorry, that probably sounds arrogant."

"No. Not at all." Even though the two of them came from different worlds, Bryce understood because he felt the same way. That was why he'd taken a job as a Web developer. He'd wanted to make it on his own terms. Not live off the rewards of his great-grandfather's real estate foresight over a hundred years ago. "It's important to make it on your own, especially if people said you couldn't."

She reached across the table and touched his hand. "You get it."

He nodded, trying not to stare at her hand. Dani's gesture was friendly, not sexual, but he enjoyed the feel of her soft skin against his. She pulled her hand back. He missed her warmth.

"I want to buy my mom a house. Nothing fancy, maybe a white picket fence. Just someplace that belongs to her. We never really had that. A home of our own."

"A worthy goal."

She nodded. "Something to work toward, that's for sure."

Sanfrandani seemed nice. She was close to her family, funny and intelligent. A guy could do a lot worse. But he couldn't forget why he was here.

*I'm a spy.*

Bryce straightened. He needed to figure out what she'd meant by that. Spying didn't always mean espionage. She might have joined the site to spy on a crush, a boyfriend or an ex.

"Why haven't you gone on more dates?" He wanted some answers. "Did you try using the compatibility matching program? The questionnaire seems thorough enough."

"Oh, it was thorough all right." Her mouth quirked. "That stupid thing took forever to fill out, with all its nitpicky and redundant questions."

He'd heard the criticism before, but the question-naire was far from stupid. "The time you spend pays out in the end."

"Let's be real." She leaned toward him. "How do you know someone else is going to fill it out as carefully as you did? They might choose an answer they think someone might want to hear."

"That's built into the algorithm and the reason for so many questions, even redundant ones. To get to the bottom of what a person needs in a relationship and a mate. Not what they think they need."

"You seem to know a lot about it."

"I work with computers," he admitted, waiting for questions to follow. So many people worked with computers in the Bay Area, yet some women wanted to know more—where do you work, what's your title, do you get stock options?—in order to gauge future earning potential.

"Poor you." She poked her fork into her waffle and swallowed a bite.

Was Sanfrandani really disinterested in him or playing hard to get? Maybe she was just hungry. That waffle looked good.

"I like computers," he said. "And with anything Internet based, there's an element of trust involved."

"Not everyone plays fair."

Bryce wasn't exactly playing fair with her. But then again, she might be guilty of the same. He was here protecting his company and his customers. He doubted her reasons would be considered honorable if she'd come under false pretenses. "Did you have a bad experience?"

"You're my first experience."

At least she was keeping her story straight. "You don't seem the shy type."

Her gaze met his. Unwavering and strong. "I'm not."

"You just haven't wanted to date anyone."

She nodded once.

Why pay the monthly membership fee then? Something with her story didn't add up. "So why did you join the site in the first place?"

"I…" She opened her mouth. Closed it. An attractive pink tinged her cheeks. "Curiosity?"

He didn't buy her answer. "Don't you want to meet somebody?"

She leaned back in her chair, eyeing him warily. "For a first date, you're awfully interested in my sex life."

Bryce grinned ruefully. "You caught me."

"Sorry."

"No, I like it."

"Like what?" Two lines formed over her nose. "That I'm abrasive?"

"Not abrasive. Confident. Willing to speak your mind and challenge me without getting all flustered." Bryce might be keeping his identity secret, but he could be honest about what he liked about her. "I find you very…"

Sanfrandani raised her chin and boldly met his gaze. "What?"

"Interesting."

She drew her brows together. "Even looking like this?"

"Yes."

"Be still my heart. That's almost as good as saying I have a great personality."

She was a tough nut to crack. Then again, he always loved a challenge. "You do have a great personality."

"Oh, boy."

"What did I say?"

"Great personality." Her eyes danced with mischief. "That's what guys say right before they say let's be friends."

"Nothing wrong with starting out as friends and seeing where things go."

She drank her mocha, feigning disinterest. Unless her indifference was real.

He found her charming in a curious sort of way. "So let's see, we've talked about dating and our families. What's next?"

"The weather?"

Bryce laughed. "Tell me about your job. Your profile says you're in sales."

"Yes, I am." She pushed up the sleeve of her sweatshirt and checked her watch. "Oh. Would you look at the time? This has been great, but I really need to be going."

"So soon?" Without answering his question. He shouldn't have been surprised.

"Yes." But the regret flickering in her eyes appeared genuine. "I'm sorry."

"Me, too." He didn't know what to make of her odd contradictions. "I don't even know your real name. I'm guessing it might be Dani, based on your user name."

She bit her lip. "Does it matter?"

Yes. No. "Not really, but I'm Bryce."

He didn't say his last name. He couldn't. One visit to Google, and she'd know exactly who he was.

Her face clouded with uneasiness. "I'm Dani."

"Thanks, Dani." He might like her, but her evasiveness had raised his suspicions. Bryce knew better than to trust her, but he wasn't ready to say goodbye just yet. He wanted to learn more about her. Who was he kidding? He wanted to see her again. "Would you like to have dinner with me? Tomorrow night?"

"I'd like that," Dani said. "But tomorrow doesn't work for me."

"Got a date?" he teased.

She wet her lips. "Actually, I do."

* * *

Blinddatebrides.com is running sixteen chat rooms, fifty-three private IM conferences, and 9289 members are online. Chat with your dating prospects now!

Private IM conference #42 (3 participants)…

Engishcrumpet: So he's attractive?

Sanfrandani: Yes. His profile picture doesn't do him justice. You can't tell how green his eyes are. Or how nice his smile is. Or see the slight bump on his nose that makes him look a little rugged.

Kangagirl: Bryce sounds yummy.

Sanfrandani: I wouldn't mind a taste.

Who was she kidding? She wouldn't mind gobbling him all up. But he appealed to her on a variety of levels, both physical as well as emotional. She'd felt a connection with him. One she wanted to explore further. If only she could…

Kangagirl: Go for it!

Englishcrumpet: Unless you already have.

Sanfrandani: I haven't. We only had coffee. I hardly know him.

Kangagirl: Sounds like you should get to know him better.

Englishcrumpet: When do you see him again?

Sanfrandani: He said he'd be in touch. But after

I told him I had another date, I doubt I'll hear back from him.

And that bothered Dani. More than she wanted to admit. He'd had a funny look on his face when she'd told him about her upcoming date. Maybe she shouldn't have told him the truth, but his dinner invitation had taken her by surprise. The entire meeting had, really. She kept replaying their conversation in her mind. Not that it mattered with her job and all.

Sanfrandani: It's no big deal. Remember, this is market research.

At least that was what Dani kept reminding herself as she had checked her in-box for the umpteenth time. Not that she expected Bryce to contact her after saying goodbye to her this morning, but on the off chance he had…

Kangagirl: You could always ask him out.
Englishcrumpet: That's a brilliant idea, Marissa.
Sanfrandani: I can't. Not unless I wanted to lie to him or tell him the truth about why I joined the site and risk losing my job. And now, with my boss wanting me to go out with any guy who contacts me, it's just too complicated.

Kangagirl: Maybe, but look at Rick and me. That was complicated. You have to remember, if it's meant to be, it'll work out.

Englishcrumpet: That's right. I never expected to fall in love again, let alone get married and have another baby. You never know how things will work out, Dani.

Kangagirl: So don't give up hope.

Dani wanted to believe her friends, yet she had her doubts. And the guilt kept building. Her life had felt like a lie for half a year now. The job, the spying, now the dating.

She thought about the man she was meeting tomorrow night for dinner. Gymguy seemed pleasant enough, but his e-mail had been more of a sales pitch about himself. He didn't mention anything about her. Nothing like…

She sighed.

Bryce.

Bryce didn't know what to do.

He tapped his pencil against his desk. The rapid tattoo on the wood matched the throbbing at his temples. He had work issues to deal with, but only one thing was on his mind—Dani.

*Actually, I do.*

She had another date. A date, he'd discovered

when he probed deeper, with another guy from Blinddatebrides.com.

He shouldn't care. He didn't care. He should be glad she was proving herself to be an ordinary client.

Except there was nothing ordinary about Dani.

Bryce couldn't stop thinking about her.

Why would she suddenly decide to go on dates after months of turning men down?

Not knowing the answer bugged him. He needed to find out what was going on. Not for his sake, but for the Web site.

And he knew how to do that.

Bryce was the founder and CEO of Blinddate-brides.com. The terms of use customers agreed to when they joined the Web site gave him permission to read whatever he wanted. He had administrative access to everything, from chat logs to messages sent between users on the site. Viewing a user's account wasn't unheard of for debugging or monitoring metrics for site usage.

Or tracking down abusers.

Or possible abusers, such as Dani.

Checking her user account made perfect sense, Bryce rationalized. Reading private e-mails for personal reasons was unethical, but as part of an ongoing investigation…

That was all he was doing. Investigating.

It wasn't as if he'd asked Grant to pull all her chat logs. He'd let the filtering system deal with those.

She'd made the date before she'd met him. Bryce had figured out that much from what she would tell him. Now he just wanted—make that needed—to know a little more.

He logged into the admin system.

Time to do a little poking around in her e-mails to see exactly what was going on with Sanfrandani.

# CHAPTER FOUR

"SEE anything you like?" asked Dani's date.

She looked over her menu at Gymguy aka Gregg.

He smiled back smugly.

Most women would like *him*, Dani supposed. His blond corporate hairstyle, tanned skin and bleached teeth reminded her of a weekend news anchor. Nice-looking, but easily forgettable once you changed the channel. Though she wasn't sure where his user name came from because he looked more on the thin and weak side than fit and strong from working out at a gym.

She glanced at her menu. "There's quite a selection."

He'd chosen a popular restaurant in Cow Hollow for dinner, although she'd suggested they meet for coffee instead. He'd even ordered an expensive wine, a bottle of Cabernet, over her objections. Maybe he wanted to impress her. Maybe he had control issues.

Maybe he was trying to get her drunk.

"The salmon with the cranberry chutney looks interesting." Her budget didn't allow splurging on expensive meals, but James had given her enough cash to cover the entire tab, including tip, so she could order whatever she wanted. One good thing about her boss—he wasn't a cheapskate. If he developed some ethics, morals and a heart, she might even like working for him. "Though the Macadamia nut-crusted halibut sounds delicious."

"I noticed that one myself." Gregg lowered his menu. "And just so there's no tug of war over the bill later, tonight is on me."

Maybe Dani had misjudged his ordering the wine and everything else. He was probably just being polite.

And she wasn't.

She couldn't blame Gregg for her not wanting to be here. It wasn't his fault she'd accepted the date under false pretenses and was feeling guilty.

How could she not when the ambience of the restaurant he'd selected oozed romance, with white linen tablecloths, candles and flowers and soft classical music playing? A tad much for a blind date, perhaps, but his choice showed he'd put some thought into where to take her.

Too bad she would rather be out with Bryce. Remembering his bright, warm eyes brought a sigh to Dani's lips. She pressed them together.

No sighing or swooning allowed. Especially over a man who hadn't e-mailed her since their coffee date. At least Gregg wanted to be with her.

"Thanks." She placed her menu on the table. "But I was planning on treating you to dinner."

Gregg's beaming smile showed two rows of perfectly white, straight teeth, but he had nothing on Bryce's easy grin. "Good thing I beat you to it."

Not really.

Dani wanted to pay. She had to pay. Or the mounting guilt might do her in.

Once upon a time, she had a great job, a new car and a one-bedroom apartment with a peek of the San Francisco Bay out her living room window and a reserved parking spot.

How had she gotten…here? Dating strangers to get information her boss wanted?

She reached past her wineglass to her water and drank.

Dani didn't want to be dating. Not Bryce or Gregg or any man. Relationships were like flesh-eating viruses that destroyed dreams and gnawed away at life plans. And when they ended you were left with nothing. She was better off without one.

"So…" Gregg raised his wineglass "…you're a lot better-looking than your profile picture."

"I hoped guys might read my profile instead of going by a photo."

"That's exactly what I did." His gaze dropped from her face to her breasts. "Smart move on my part, that's for sure."

Darn it. Dani had worn loose-fitting clothes—a skirt, blouse and sweater—to hide her curves, but he'd somehow seen enough to capture his attention. She should have worn the baggy sweats instead.

Gregg stared at her chest, focusing on her breasts as if he had see-through clothing vision. "Though you'd probably get more takers if you mentioned you had such nice melons in your profile."

Dani choked. Coughed. Wiped her mouth with her napkin.

O-kay. So much for him being polite.

But she knew how to deal with men like Gregg. Knew all too well.

With her napkin back on her lap, she straightened. "Stick to the Macadamia nuts, Gregg. You can't handle the melons."

His mouth gaped. He closed it.

"I sure would like to if you'll give me the chance." Gregg leaned over the table toward her, and she noticed how his eyes looked beady like a sewer rat's. "My place is walking distance from here. Why don't we skip dinner, head over there and go straight to dessert?"

She bit back a sigh. So typical.

And to think she'd been feeling guilty for using

him to get information when he wanted to use her for sex. At least Bryce had been a gentleman when he was out with her.

Gregg raised an eyebrow and puckered his lips slightly. "You know you want to go back to my apartment with me."

Jerk. She bypassed the water and sipped from her wineglass. No sense wasting an expensive bottle.

Or the opportunity. Although lowering herself to his level left a bitter taste in her mouth.

Consider it market research, she told herself. Or morbid curiosity. "Do you do this a lot?"

"Depends on your definition of a lot, but I'm sure I could squeeze you in with my busy schedule." He sipped his wine. "We will be so good together."

She should have gone out with Bryce instead of this wannabe who gave players a bad name. "In bed, you mean?"

"Where else?" Gregg took another drink. "Women might say they are looking for a long-term commitment on their profiles, but secretly they're looking for an adventure. All they need is the right man to lead the way."

"You've figured this out on your own?"

"All by myself." That smug smile of his returned. "Are you ready for an adventure, Dani?"

Gregg reached across the table, past the flicker-ing votive candle, past the bud vase containing a

Gerbera daisy, past her hand, to stroke the juncture of her breasts with his fingertip.

Disgust sent her flying back. She nearly fell. As she jerked to her feet, her chair crashed to the floor.

The restaurant was dead quiet. Customers stared. The waitstaff, too.

She didn't care. "What are you doing?"

"Giving you what you want," he said.

"What I want?" Dani's blood pressure soared. His words took her straight back to high school, where the boys had elbowed each other and propositioned her when she'd walked by. She'd ignored their taunts even though it hurt because she'd wanted to be part of the popular crowd. She was older, wiser now. No need to try and fit in with people she'd never liked in the first place. "What I want is for you to crawl back into the hole you slithered out of."

"You're a feisty one, aren't you?" He raised his eyebrows up and down, as if performing a bizarre mating call. "Women who play hard to get are usually good in bed."

"You'll never know." She picked up her glass of water and tossed the contents on his lap. "That should cool you off."

Gregg jumped up, grabbed a napkin and patted himself. "Why, you little—"

"Is there a problem?"

The male voice came from behind. She turned. Bryce.

Surprise skittered through Dani, along with a flash of joy. Her mouth went dry. She'd been thinking about Bryce all evening and wanting to see him. Now he was here, looking all gorgeous in a brown suit, and concerned about her, as if she'd summoned him from those same thoughts.

Dani gloried in the moment, a wide grin on her face.

And then she remembered.

She wasn't alone. Her cheeks burned.

Dani glanced at a red-faced Gregg, frantically drying the front of his pants and muttering to himself.

"Are you okay?" Bryce asked.

The tenderness of his voice alleviated some of her humiliation. She stared up at him. So handsome. So strong.

He had a looking-for-a-fight gleam in his eyes. His wanting to protect pleased her. Feminine power surged. And then she remembered the brawl scene from *Bridget Jones's Diary*.

Oh, no. All she needed was two yuppies who didn't know how to fight duking it out over her in a nice restaurant to top off the night. No way could she allow that to happen.

Sure, she appreciated Bryce wanting to come to her assistance, except this wasn't a dark alley or the backseat of some guy's car. She had this situation under control. "I'm fine."

"Well, I'm not." Gregg frowned. The water stain on his pants made him look as if he'd wet himself. "I should have known a chick with such a nice rack would be nothing but a tease."

A vein throbbed at Bryce's jaw. "Why don't we step outside?"

Okay, she might not need rescuing and she sure didn't want anyone fighting over her, but the way he'd challenged Gregg was totally romantic. Totally Austen hero-worthy, too.

Dani bit back a sigh.

Gregg must have agreed because he seemed to shrink before her eyes. He took two steps backward. "You want to fight me?"

"No," Bryce said. "I want her to have more room when she kicks your scrawny wet ass."

Her heart melted.

Gregg's startled gaze darted between Bryce and her. A second later, he bolted from the restaurant.

She laughed. "I never realized I was that terrifying."

"You have no idea."


Outside the restaurant, streetlamps illuminated the crowded sidewalk. A breeze carried the salty scent of the bay. Dani stood next to Bryce.

A foghorn sounded. The cyclical blares reminded

her she was no longer the dirt-poor girl she'd once been, the housekeeper's daughter with boobs too big and hips too round. The girl no boy respected, but every boy wanted.

The memory sent a shiver down her spine. Dani crossed her arms over her.

Bryce shrugged off his jacket and placed it around her shoulders. "This will keep you warm."

He was doing a good enough job heating her up himself. Standing there with shadows cast on his face, he looked dangerous and sexy, but acted more like a knight than a rake.

Smiling, she buttoned his coat. Not only because of the cold, but because she wanted to feel closer to him. This might be her only chance. She wasn't going to miss out. "Thanks."

"You're welcome."

"I can't believe you were at the restaurant." Dani breathed in his soap and water scent on the jacket. Funny, but for some reason she thought he would wear cologne. "What a coincidence."

Bryce stared at a yellow cab driving by. "Yeah, I ordered takeout, but decided to eat here instead of going home alone."

Hope fluttered. He wasn't on a date. She shouldn't care. She didn't care. Okay, maybe a little.

"But you had it covered," Bryce continued. "You didn't need my help with that guy."

"It was nice to have backup."

He bowed. "Big brother at your service."

She gave a quick curtsy. "We made a good team."

"We did." Bryce glanced back at the restaurant. "But what went on in there should have never happened."

She waited for the familiar litany to begin. That she was the one to blame when guys got carried away. That it was her fault. That she had been asking for it.

"The guy was a total jerk. You deserve to be treated so much better than that. He should be kicked off Blinddatebrides.com for his actions."

Dani felt a familiar melting of her heart, the same way she'd felt when he'd stuck up for her a few minutes ago. His anger seemed so sincere, so real. And though he had bad things, valid criticisms, to say about Gregg, Bryce wasn't using her experience to talk himself up. She respected that.

Him.

She wanted to hug Bryce. To thank him. To hold him.

He was different, a gentleman.

Someone who looked beyond the surface to see the person underneath.

Someone who wasn't afraid to step forward.

Someone who cared.

About her.

Her pulse raced as if she'd just completed a competition round in the ring. "I'm going to file a complaint with the site."

"Do," he encouraged. "His account can be suspended."

"Unfortunately, he'll go to another dating site and do the same thing with other women," she said. "What we've experienced is the dark side of online dating. Some people, and not just men, only want sex and are willing to do or say anything to get it."

"Blinddatebrides.com is for those people wanting a serious relationship." Bryce sounded frustrated, annoyed.

"Players and liars are everywhere. Even on Blinddatebrides.com."

"It shouldn't be like that." Bryce sounded so idealistic. "Those people should sign up for one of the casual sex sites like Hookamate.com instead."

Dani winced. His words were like a slap to the face. Hearing Bryce say the truth embarrassed her. Worse, she agreed with him. But nothing could change about that until she found a new job. She only wondered whether he would want to see her again if he knew the truth about where she worked and what she did.

"Not everyone reads the terms of use," Dani said. "Or cares."

"They should care." His eyes practically caressed her, and she sucked in a breath. "I care."

Uh-oh. Her mouth went dry. Her heart beat faster.

Bryce was someone she could maybe care about. Maybe have something real with, but not this way.

She swallowed around the lump of emotion lodged in her throat.

Not under these circumstances.

She had to get away from him. Now. Before she messed up having any chance with him in the future. "I should be going home so you can get back to your dinner."

"I finished eating."

His gaze locked with hers. Hypnotic.

A connection seemed to draw him to her.

They stood there, silent, staring at each other as if entranced. The noise of the city disappeared, consumed by the night. It was only her and Bryce.

And that felt…right.

No, not right.

Dani fought hard to break his spell. She didn't know enough about him. And he didn't know the truth about her, which made it nowhere close to being right.

She looked away.

"It didn't look as if you ate dinner in there," Bryce said. "Would you like to get something to eat?"

Yes. No. Life wasn't fair.

Why had she met him now?

She found Bryce to be intelligent, nice and totally hot. He was exactly the kind of man she wanted to meet in, say, five years, when she had her career established and was ready to make a commitment. She wasn't ready for that at the moment, with her life in such disarray.

"Thanks, but I need to go home."

Far, far away from the sexy and attractive Bryce.

"I'll walk you to your car."

She'd had to sell her car after she'd got laid off. "I took the bus."

He swept his hand through his hair. "Would you like a ride home?"

What a stupid move.

Some idiot had accosted Dani, and Bryce had asked her to get into a car with him, someone she barely knew. He wanted to kick himself. That was what he got for acting impulsively.

But he hadn't been able to help himself.

Dani brought out his impatience. Bryce didn't like that.

Nor did he like how she had been constantly on his mind since having coffee and how he couldn't stop staring at her now.

But damn, she cleaned up well, even if her clothes still looked a couple of sizes too big. If he weren't careful, he was going to blow this.

The investigation, he meant.

"I can call you a cab," Bryce offered.

"I take the bus all the time."

"It's late," he countered. "My treat."

"I'm a big girl."

"I know you can handle situations after seeing you in action. But you shouldn't have to deal with anything else tonight."

The determined set of her jaw reminded him of his sister when she wasn't going to take no for an answer. Bryce knew when to surrender.

"If your heart is set on riding the bus home, I'll walk you to the stop."

That was the least Bryce could do. He felt guilty for using information from her e-mails. She'd called his being at the restaurant a coincidence. Good thing she didn't know that no chance or luck had been involved in his witnessing her date-gone-bad.

Frustration gnawed at him. Bryce hated how guys like Gregg could slip through the system without being weeded out. He felt protective over Dani, the way he did with all his customers, and right now a part of him wanted to hold her. Though he normally didn't hug clients.

A hug would probably go over as well as his offer of a ride home had so he kept his hands to himself.

"I'm sure the last thing you want to do is get into the car with a total stranger. Or a player or a liar." Bryce remembered what she'd said. "Not that I'm strange or any of those other things. But you wouldn't know that."

"I wouldn't," she admitted. "It's hard to separate the good guys from the psychos these days."

He fell in step with her. "Unless one happens to be carrying around an axe or a chainsaw."

"That would give them away." She walked toward the street corner. "Still, I can't imagine you wielding a knife with a crazed look in your eyes."

"Once you get to know me, you'll realize I'm harmless."

Dani stopped at the corner and hit the crosswalk button. Traffic zipped across the intersection. "When I get to know you?"

Bryce nodded. "That's the only way I won't be a stranger to you. You never know when you might need another ride home."

"You've got this all figured out."

"I'm working on it."

"What did you have in mind?" she asked.

She was tempted. He could hear it in her voice. Good.

"Dinner and conversation," he said.

The light changed. The walk sign illuminated. She stepped off the curb. "As long as nothing else happening will be assumed."

"I never assume anything." Bryce didn't want to let her go without getting a commitment from her. He wanted to know when he would see her again. "How does Friday sound?"

"This Friday?" she asked.

He nodded. Waited. Reminded himself that patience was a virtue.

"Okay," she said after what seemed like hours but was only minutes. Probably seconds. "That sounds good."

They reached the other side of the street. "Great."

A bus pulled to the curb, the brakes squealing as it rolled to a stop. The door opened.

"Are you sure you don't want to take a taxi?" he asked.

"Thanks, but I'm comfortable taking the bus." She started removing his coat. "Your jacket—"

"Keep it," he said. "You don't want to get cold. Give it back to me on Friday."

She stepped onto the bus and glanced back at him. "Thanks for everything."

Bryce hated to see her go. "You never know who you'll run into on Muni. E-mail me when you get home, if you get the chance."

"Will do." She smiled down at him. "Bye."

A disturbing feeling settled in the bottom of his stomach. "Goodnight, Dani."

An hour later, Bryce stared at his laptop monitor. No e-mail from Dani yet. He'd even checked to see if she'd logged into the Web site. She hadn't.

His fingers tensed over the keyboard.

Maybe he should call her. She'd listed her phone number when she'd registered for the site. And then he remembered. Blinddatebrides.com had her number. Not him.

He glanced at the clock.

What was taking Dani so long to get home?

Worry seemed premature. Still…

Bryce should have called a cab for her, but he hadn't been thinking straight. Not since he'd met Dani for coffee…

Had it only been yesterday?

He felt as if he'd known her longer.

Still, his interest in her made zero sense given what he knew about her and what he didn't.

Yes, Dani was pretty, but she wasn't the most beautiful woman he'd ever met. Tonight she'd worn her hair in a ponytail, but had bypassed the makeup again. He liked the fresh-faced natural look. And that subtle perfume of hers—vanilla with a hint of something else, something exotic—smelled so good. He wouldn't mind waking up to that scent on his pillow.

But cyberspace was full of players and liars. Dani had said so herself. And thieves and spies, he reminded himself. Was she one of them?

Bryce didn't think so.

He recalled her look of surprise when she'd first seen him at the restaurant. Her smile had told him she'd been relieved and happy. Not even an award-winning actress could fake the kind of sincerity she'd shown tonight.

Dani was probably a timid dater. Okay, she had been able to take care of Gymguy on her own, but he couldn't imagine her as a scammer or spy, in spite of what she'd said. Taken out of context, almost anything could sound suspicious. And that made his motives for following her seem suspect.

Still, he would remain cautious.

He couldn't forget his responsibility in all this—make sure no one caused trouble on the Web site. Blinddatebrides.com was his priority. No getting sidetracked allowed.

The phone rang. The only person he wanted to talk to didn't have his number. Bryce noticed the name on the caller I.D. Caitlin. She wouldn't call at this hour without a reason.

Bryce snatched up the receiver. "Hey, sis. What's going on?"

"Mother doesn't want Father to bring his newest girlfriend to the engagement party." Caitlin sniffled as if she'd been crying. "And she wants me to be the one to tell him. If I do that, he might not come. He might not win any father of the year awards, but I want him there, Bryce."

The crack in his sister's voice squeezed his heart. The ripples from their parents' divorce hadn't lessened over the years. He still remembered the years of yelling, screaming and breaking things that had led up to their split. "Don't worry. By the time the party rolls around, the girlfriend will probably be his new wife."

"That's what I told Mother," Caitlin said. "She got even more upset. You'd think, after twenty-some years apart, with almost a dozen marriages between them, they'd be able to get over it."

Bryce stepped around a stack of newspapers he needed to take out to the recycling bin and sat on the couch. "I'll talk to her."

"Thanks." Gratitude filled her voice. "I knew I could count on you."

"That's what big brothers are for."

"Are you okay?" Caitlin asked. "You sound...I don't know...different."

He glanced at his laptop, sitting on the coffee table. "I'm waiting for something."

"You've never been good at waiting. Remember on Christmas Eve when you woke up in the middle of the night and wanted to open presents?"

"I was ten."

"And now you're thirty-two. Not too much has changed."

"Thanks, sis."

"Anytime," Caitlin said. "So what are you waiting for at this hour?"

"An e-mail."

"I was hoping it was a woman," she admitted.

He wasn't about to go there. "Sorry."

"Don't forget, you need to find a date to the engagement party or you'll be fighting off all the single women there. And a few of the married ones, too."

"I can handle them—" he thought about Dani "—though I may have a lead on a possible date."

"Who?"

"A woman."

"Give me a name. Something." Caitlin sighed, but he would guess she was smiling now. "Come on, Bryce. You saying 'date' without making it sound like a four-letter word is huge."

"There isn't anything to tell right now." Inviting Dani to the party probably wasn't a good idea given the circumstances. "But if the situation changes I'll let you know."

"Promise?" Caitlin sounded more like a little girl than a bride-to-be.

Bryce knew his sister would call their mother about his potential "date." Maybe that would take some pressure off Caitlin and whether their father and his girlfriend could attend the party. "I promise I'll let you know if I ask someone, but don't get your hopes up."

"Are you kidding? Hope is already overflowing."

"It's not that big a deal."

"Oh, yes, it is," Caitlin countered. "The fact

you're actually considering getting away from your computer long enough to meet and go out with a woman is almost miraculous."

Bryce frowned. "You make me sound like a total geek."

"If the pocket protector fits…"

His computer dinged. He glanced at his in-box and saw an e-mail from Dani. Finally. "I gotta go."

"That e-mail you're waiting for is from her, isn't it?"

He clicked on the message. "Goodnight, sis."

"It is." Caitlin laughed. "Goodnight, big brother. Keep me posted on what's going on. And don't forget. You promised."

The line disconnected. Bryce turned off the phone. The e-mail appeared on his screen. He pulled his computer onto his lap and read.

To: "Bigbrother" <bigbrother@blinddate-brides.com>
From: "Sanfrandani" <sanfrandani@blinddate-brides.com>
Subject: Made it
I'm in my apartment though there were moments I doubted whether I'd make it back or not. A group of mimes boarded at Divisadero and decided I needed to be entertained. Not a smart decision on their part. I would rather face a psychopath wielding an axe than a clown. -d

To: "Sanfrandani" <sanfrandani@blinddate-brides.com>
From: "Bigbrother" <bigbrother@blinddate-brides.com>
Subject: RE: Made it
Glad to hear you survived the trip in spite of the mischievous mimes. Sorry I wasn't there to see it. Note to self: leave face paint at home on Friday night.

To: "Bigbrother" <bigbrother@blinddate-brides.com>
From: "Sanfrandani" <sanfrandani@blinddate-brides.com>
Subject: RE: RE: Made it
You didn't miss much except for seeing a grown mime cry.
Good call on the face paint or you'd be spending the evening alone and in tears.

To: "Sanfrandani" <sanfrandani@blinddate-brides.com>
From: "Bigbrother" <bigbrother@blinddate-brides.com>
Subject: RE: RE: RE: Made it
Wouldn't want that.
Meet me under the rotunda of the Palace of Fine Arts at six-thirty on Friday. I'll bring dinner and we can have a picnic.

To: "Bigbrother" <bigbrother@blinddate-brides.com>

From: "Sanfrandani" <sanfrandani@blinddate-brides.com>

Subject: RE: RE: RE: RE: Made it

What can I bring?

To: "Sanfrandani" <sanfrandani@blinddate-brides.com>

From: "Bigbrother" <bigbrother@blinddate-brides.com>

Subject: RE: RE: RE: RE: RE: Made it

I won't suggest dessert.

To: "Bigbrother" <bigbrother@blinddate-brides.com>

From: "Sanfrandani" <sanfrandani@blinddate-brides.com

Subject: RE: RE: RE: RE: RE: RE: Made it

I have no problem providing dessert as long as it's not assumed to be me.

P.S. Looking forward to Friday.

Bryce smiled. So was he.

## CHAPTER FIVE

NOT a date, Dani reminded herself as she adjusted the shoulder strap of her bag and walked along a path at the Palace of Fine Arts. That was all she had to remember tonight and she'd be fine.

Marissa had e-mailed, calling the not-a-date with Bryce strictly another information-gathering meeting. Grace had agreed in an e-mail of her own, suggesting Dani keep the conversation tonight focused on Blinddatebrides.com and his online dating experiences.

Good advice from both her friends, except for one thing…

Dani wanted this to be a real date.

Not that she wanted a boyfriend per se, but she wanted to see Bryce, to spend time with him. And, to be honest, she couldn't care less if Blinddatebrides.com even came up in the conversation.

On her right, two swans swam across the lake. Elegant and graceful, a pair mated for life.

She watched them, feeling a little envious. Not that she wanted a husband in the near future, if ever, but the idea of something lasting a lifetime was beginning to appeal to her heart and soul. Nothing in her life had ever lasted long.

Was it so horrible to want forever? Or to want to go on a date with Bryce?

He was a really nice guy. She enjoyed his company. No sense pretending she didn't because of what might happen.

One date wouldn't stop her from finding a new job or moving forward with her life. One date wouldn't make her dependent on someone. One date wouldn't change anything.

Dani walked to the exact center of the Romanesque rotunda and looked up at the top of the dome.

The vastness of the structure made her feel so small, so inconsequential. The way she'd felt ever since being laid off from her dream job. She hated feeling this way, floundering and frustrated and living a lie. That wasn't the kind of person she'd strived to be all these years. Dani wanted to make something of herself, make a difference, but she felt as if she were standing on a playground merry-go-round being spun around by a group of mean kids with no way to get off.

She wanted off. Out.

Dani was tired of things being out of her control,

of struggling to check the next item off her to-do list. She needed to lighten up and have fun. Tonight with Bryce would be a good start.

So might something else. She remembered a piece of trivia she'd read about this place on a San Francisco tourist Web site.

Dani clapped her hands together once. The sound echoed perfectly through the dome.

"I used to do that when I was a kid."

She jumped, startled by Bryce's voice. He looked handsome in a green polo shirt and khaki pants. With his casually styled hair and steady grin, he reminded her more of a fashion model than a computer geek. Except for the paper bag he held.

"You don't have to be a kid to do it," she challenged.

His gaze, intense and unwavering, met hers. "Step aside."

She did.

Bryce handed her the bag. The scent of rosemary wafted out. He positioned himself at the center, looked up at the dome's ceiling and clapped. The sharp sound echoed through the rotunda. "Satisfied?"

"Very."

"Me, too."

The way he studied her made her think she'd gotten a smudge of dirt on her face. "What?"

"You wore your hair down."

She tucked her hair behind her ears. "I couldn't find my bandana."

"Your hair's longer than I thought it would be."

Dani couldn't tell if her hair length was a good thing. Not that his opinion mattered. Much. "I keep thinking I should cut it and go for one of those trendy new styles."

"Your hair looks great the way it is," he said. "You shouldn't change it unless you really want to."

He sounded as if he'd had this conversation before. And then she remembered. Caitlin. "Spoken like a true big brother."

Bryce shrugged, looking a little embarrassed and a lot more like his profile picture—that shy, easy to hurt guy Dani had imagined.

"It's sound advice," she added. "Thanks."

"Just don't ask me to braid your hair." He shivered. "I still have nightmares over that one. Caitlin, too."

Dani laughed. "Don't worry, I can braid my hair myself."

He made an exaggerated swipe at his brow. "Good, I was worried for a minute."

She was a little worried herself.

Bryce was too cute, the kind of guy you wanted to take home. Intelligent, nice, attractive, funny. Her friends would like him. Her mother and sisters, too.

Not a date, she reminded herself.

"Nice outfit," he said.

"Thanks." She'd chosen a nice pair of brown pants, a blue blouse and a cropped lightweight jacket. Not super-fitted clothes, but these showed a few curves. She'd considered wearing her baggy sweats or another of the loose-fitting outfits hanging in the back of her closet and forgoing makeup again, but something inside of her had revolted at the thought of playing the role of ugly duckling again. She wanted Bryce to see her for who she was.

Inside and out.

His gaze, slow and appreciative, didn't stop at her breasts, but ran the length of her and back up again. "Your shirt brings out the blue of your eyes."

She drew back. "You know what color my eyes are?"

"You sound surprised."

"I am. Most guys…"

"Most guys," he prompted.

She might as well be honest. "Most guys never see beyond my bra cup size."

He shrugged. "Their loss."

Dani was used to men liking her body, not her. She was always seen as a trophy, a piece of arm candy. She bit her lip, not sure what to make of Bryce.

"Close your eyes," he ordered.

She did.

"What color are my eyes?"

"Green."

"Correct," he said as she opened her eyes. "Guess you're not just interested in my cup size, either. So we're even."

Dani wasn't sure about that. She felt off balance, as if her not-so-neat little world had been spun in yet another direction by him. She didn't like the feeling.

"Ready to eat?" he asked.

"Please. I worked through lunch and am starving," she said. "Whatever you brought smells delicious."

"It does smell good, but I can't take credit for the food. I picked up dinner at a little place on Chestnut."

Bryce led her from the rotunda to a path leading around the lake. "I put down a blanket to claim a spot. With nice weather like this, I didn't want to take any chances."

"It is a beautiful day." She tilted her head toward the sky so the sun's rays could kiss her cheeks. "Though I'm not sure there are any bad picnic spots here."

"True," he admitted. "That's why I like this place. Even with the tourists snapping pictures like crazy, it's still peaceful."

"I know." His words echoed how she felt and made her feel warm and fuzzy inside. "I've always thought of this place as somewhere to escape from the hectic pulse of life in the city. And you never know what you'll see. One time they were filming a television show."

He stopped at a grassy area where a blue blanket was spread out. "Here we are."

Dani stared across the water. The two swans she'd seen earlier were still floating on the lake, but this time they had the "palace" as the backdrop behind them. "A veritable feast for the eyes with the lake, plants and architecture."

"It's kind of like stepping back to ancient times with the Corinthian Columns."

"And the Roman-inspired rotunda. All that's missing are gladiators and deities." She looked at Bryce. "Thanks for choosing such a lovely location for a picnic."

"You're welcome," he said. "This spot actually has a lot of sentimental value to me."

Warning bells sounded in her head. Dani bit back a sigh. She had a feeling what was going to come next—a story about Bryce's ex-girlfriend who he used to bring here before she'd done him wrong. Dani didn't have much experience with that but, to be honest, she'd rather listen to him talk about an ex than deal with the I-want-you-for-your-body dates who usually asked her out.

She plopped onto the blanket, ready to hear his woeful tale. "Sentimental how?"

"I had a nanny who claimed bluebird days demanded picnics. She would have our cook make us a picnic, sometimes two, if she planned on keeping us outside the entire time." Bryce patted the blanket. "This was one of her favorite picnic spots."

The affection in his voice brought a smile to Dani's face. "Sounds like you had fun with her."

"We did." He pulled white boxes from the sack. "She was one Caitlin and I were sad to lose."

"You had a lot of nannies?" Dani asked.

Nodding, he pulled out plates and utensils. "My parents paid them well, but the nannies earned every penny of their salary dealing with my mother and father, not us."

Dani toyed with a blade of grass. "Leaving your kids with someone for an extended period has to be hard on parents."

"I wouldn't do it."

His adamant tone surprised her, but didn't seem to affect him in the slightest. He placed asparagus spears with salad on one side of the plate and a scoop of couscous on the other. A chicken breast covered with mushrooms in a light sauce went in the center.

"Do you plan on being a stay-at-home dad or having your wife give up her career?" she asked, thinking about her mother and all she'd given up for her marriage and children.

"I haven't given much thought to marriage or having a family. It's not something I'm interested in right now." Bryce handed her a plate. "But I do know when I was a kid and got hurt or was upset, I wanted my mother or father. Not my nanny. I'd rather not have to go that route with children of my own."

"Some people have no choice." Dani stared at her plate, overflowing with food, and remembered the times when she didn't have as much. "When I was in sixth grade, we moved to Los Angeles. My sisters and I would go to day care—they called it after-care, when school got out until about six o'clock. We were there in the morning before school started, too. It was hard on all of us, but I think most especially my mom. She didn't want to have to put us there for so long each day, but she had no choice because of her job."

"Sounds like you all did what you had to do."

She nodded, scooping up a forkful of couscous. "That was the first time any of us started and finished a grade at the same school."

"Did you live in Los Angeles a long time?"

"Just a year." Dani shook her head as she swallowed. "The company downsized and my mom lost her job so we moved on."

"I've lived in San Francisco my entire life. Well, except for college. My mother still lives in the same house where I grew up."

"Wow. I can only imagine how wonderful that must be." She inhaled deeply, caught up in her dream of home ownership. "I would love to put down roots like that and never have to move again."

"Aren't you a little young for wanting that?"

Oops. She didn't want him to get the wrong idea. "I should have added someday. That's not in the plan right now. But still, you are so lucky."

His gaze locked on hers. "I feel...fortunate."

Dani was used to male attention, but Bryce wasn't focused on her chest. If anything, his watchful eyes seemed to pierce straight into her soul, to see not only her dreams, but her heart and her secrets.

She shifted position on the blanket, angling away from him slightly. "Dinner is delicious. Excellent choice of food."

"Thanks, but I just realized I haven't been a good host," he said. "I forgot to offer you a drink. I have white wine, a Chardonnay or sparkling mineral water, lime-flavored."

Her favorites. "Did you check my profile page before going shopping?"

"Of course." He grinned. "If you'd been vegan, this dinner menu would have been a flop. So what's your poison tonight?"

Water was the smart choice, but she didn't care. "Wine, please."

He uncorked the bottle. "Did you read my profile?"

Over and over again, the same way she had obsessively been checking her e-mail since he'd first contacted her, but she didn't want to tell Bryce that. "I may have skimmed your profile a couple of times. I noticed baseball seemed to be a common theme to yours."

"And Jane Austen yours." He poured the wine into glasses. "I thought about wearing a flowing white shirt."

"How long did you consider that? A second?"

"Try a nanosecond." He handed her a glass. "Cheers."

"Cheers." Dani tapped her glass against his. The chime hung in the air. She took a sip. "Great. But I thought you preferred red wine."

"Red doesn't go as well with chicken," he explained. "You must have done a little more than skim my profile if you remember what kind of wine I liked."

She ate another piece of chicken. "Yum."

"Trying to change the subject?"

"Yes." She wiped her mouth with a napkin. "Do you mind?"

A devilish gleam flashed in his eyes. "Not this time."

Did that mean he wanted to see her again?

Excitement shot through her at the possibility. She forced herself to calm down. One date. That was all this could be even if her heart might disagree. "Looking at our profiles, hearing how we grew up, we're very different."

He shrugged. "Everybody is different. But the compatibility program says we're a match."

It was her turn to shrug.

"That's right." Bryce raised his glass to his lips. "You don't believe in the matching program."

She remembered the "match" page where you could check to see who the computer thought you were most compatible with. She had visited there once to capture screen shots, analyze the information and present a report to James. "I didn't realize that's how you found me."

She cringed. Her words made it sound as if she'd been lost and needed a man—Bryce—to find her.

He didn't seem to notice. "There are lots of ways to find people on the Web site."

No kidding. Just look at her.

Dani swirled her glass. She felt like the wine spinning around inside. Everything happening in her life was out of her control. Waiting for James to tell her she could stop spying and going out on dates. Hoping another company would want to hire her so she could start afresh. Wishing things could be different right this moment.

She wanted to take action, change things now, but had no idea how to start.

Bryce refilled their glasses.

If only she could tell him the truth about working for Hookamate.com and what her job required her to do.

But she couldn't.

She couldn't risk losing her job.

Dani's family counted on her financial support. Her youngest sister's fall tuition would be due soon as well as her mother's health insurance premium. Nothing had changed since lack of money six months ago had forced Dani to take the position at Hookamate.com.

But the least she could give Bryce was her gratitude.

"Tonight has been wonderful," Dani said. "Thanks for going to so much trouble."

"It wasn't any trouble."

A comfortable silence descended as they finished their dinner. A breeze rustled the leaves of nearby trees. An older couple strolled hand in hand along the path. They glanced her way and smiled.

Dani wondered if they thought she and Bryce were a romantic couple or if they could tell this was the first dinner they'd shared together. Probably the only dinner they'd ever share. She sipped her wine.

As Bryce put things back into the bag, three white limousines pulled up to the curb. The doors opened and laughter filled the air. Members of a wedding party piled out of the cars. Eight, nine… They kept coming. Bridesmaids dressed in lavender full-length gowns and groomsmen in black tuxedos with tails. Fourteen in total. Not counting the bride and groom.

Dani stared in disbelief. "That's a huge wedding party."

"Either they come from a big family or have money to burn."

"Or both."

The bride's gown was a billowy confection of tulle and silk. Three of the bridesmaids held up the dress to keep the hem from touching the floor. Dani thought about Marissa and Grace.

"They should get some nice photos with this lighting," Dani said. The sun shone high in the sky, even though it had to be past eight by now.

She removed her cell phone from her bag and snapped a picture of the wedding party as they posed for the photographer.

"You know," Bryce said, "a guy could get the wrong idea of his date snapping pictures of wedding parties."

"Nothing nefarious. I'm not a wedding junkie or a bride wannabe," she admitted. "The photo is for my two online friends Grace and Marissa. We met in the newcomers chat on Blinddatebrides.com and have stayed in touch ever since."

"They are the ones you mentioned before."

She was pleased he remembered. "Yes. I've been trying to talk them into coming to visit me, but they are so busy with their own lives—and now loves— I don't think it's going to happen anytime soon. Maybe this picture will whet their appetite for a personal tour of San Francisco."

"My sister plans to have wedding pictures taken here."

Dani wasn't surprised. This place was popular with bridal parties for a reason. "Wedding photos here would be lovely."

"Agree, but the logistics are turning into a nightmare and causing arguments between my mother and sister, even though the wedding isn't until next year." He sipped his wine. "Caitlin wants to have photos taken before the ceremony so the wedding party can go to the reception without delay, but my mother says it's bad luck for a groom to see the bride before the wedding so they must do the pictures afterward."

Dani knew nothing about wedding planning except for what she'd picked up from Marissa and Grace. "Couldn't they do pictures the day before?"

"My mother doesn't think Mark should see Caitlin in her wedding gown. Period."

"Google it."

"Excuse me?" Bryce asked.

"Find out in what percentage of divorces did the groom see the bride before the wedding ceremony. That will either prove your sister's point or your mother's and they won't have to argue anymore."

"That's…brilliant."

"More like common sense, but thanks. It's not often I'm called brilliant."

"Then you're hanging with the wrong crowd."

Being with Bryce was so easy. Conversation flowed as easily as the wine. Being quiet didn't feel awkward or uncomfortable. He felt like an old friend, not a stranger she'd met only a few days ago online.

As he packed away the food, she handed him her plate.

"Relax," he said. "I've got it."

Dani couldn't remember the last time she'd felt so…pampered. She watched a row of turtles, a mother and her babies, swim across the lake. Bryce definitely knew what he was doing. But he didn't act like a player. Still, she couldn't help but wonder if he took every woman he went out with here. "Do you take all your dates on picnics?"

Not exactly subtle, but she wanted to know the answer.

"I don't," he admitted. "The last one was…maybe four years ago. But a woman who wears a bandana seemed like the type who might enjoy a picnic."

He sounded genuine. Dani wanted to believe him. Just because she wasn't being truthful didn't mean he was dishonest. "I do like picnics, though I haven't been on a real one like this since college. The other times were just brown bagging it and sitting on the grass."

"Then it was time for both of us to do this the right way."

Hair fell over Bryce's eyes as he finished cleaning up. Dani longed to push the strands back into place, to touch his face, to kiss him.

Maybe it was time. And not only for a picnic.

She smiled. "Are you ready for dessert?"

"These are sinfully good."

"Not sinful." Dani's smile reached her eyes, raising Bryce's temperature a degree or two. "Criminal, maybe."

No way could a woman who looked as hot as Dani did tonight and cooked delicious candies be a spy. Bryce picked up another one of her homemade bonbons. "I need more evidence before I can make a final verdict."

Lying on the blanket and resting on his elbows, he bit through the bittersweet chocolate covering to the softer Tiramisu inside. The flavors exploded in his mouth.

Sweet, moist, rich.

Like the cook herself? Bryce wouldn't mind finding out.

She watched him. "What's the verdict?"

"The calories are criminal, but worth it."

Dani beamed.

Bryce liked how a simple comment or compliment pleased her so much. She wasn't like other women he'd dated, who wanted to eat at the newest restaurants and go to the hippest clubs. Dani seemed content to be with him, no matter where that might be—a park, sidewalk, café. And when he was with her everything cluttering his brain seemed to magically disappear.

He wasn't in the market for a girlfriend, but he could get used to this. Her.

As she picked up a bonbon, her hair shifted forward. With a flip of her head, she sent the hair back behind her shoulder. The movement was subtle yet sexy, especially with the slight bounce of her breasts.

He reached for his wineglass.

"I haven't made bonbons in a while," Dani said. "I forgot how good they are."

She raised the white chocolate-covered candy to her mouth. Her pink lips parted, then closed around the bonbon.

Heat rushed through Bryce's veins. He jerked his gaze away from her and focused on the lake. He'd rather stare at her full lips or sensuous curves, but he didn't want her to compare him to the other men she'd dated. Guys like that jerk from the other night or the ones who didn't remember her eyes were a spectacular shade of blue.

"My compliments to the chef."

She bowed her head.

He picked up another. "Bet you have to know how to boil water to make these."

"That skill might come in handy, but it's not necessary," she explained. "They are easy to make unless you mind getting dirty. By the time you're finished, your fingers will be covered in chocolate sauce."

Bryce grinned. "I don't mind dirty, especially if chocolate is involved."

"If you're interested in learning how to make them, I'll show you."

"Sure." Dani and chocolate together. That was a no-brainer combination. "But I'll warn you now, I'm not much of a cook. I grill but that's the extent of my cooking talent. It's kind of a family joke."

"So you weren't kidding about boiling water?"

"I can do a little more that that, but I avoid recipes requiring oil and frying."

"Were flames involved?" Dani asked.

"Fire, smoke, a call to 9-1-1," he admitted.

Her eyes widened. "What happened?"

He gave a half-shrug, still embarrassed after all these years. "I tried to make French fries one day when the cook was sick. Unfortunately, I made two critical errors. I took the telephone to my mother, who was in another room, while frying. I also left the bag of potatoes sitting on the counter right next to the gas stove top."

"Uh-oh."

"The fire investigator wasn't sure which caught fire first, the oil or the plastic. By the time I returned to the kitchen, both were fully engaged in flames and the room covered in thick smoke. My mother and sister ran in while I was trying to put out the fire. I kept trying to remember what I'd learned about fires. One phrase kept running through my mind so I yelled it, 'Stop, drop and roll.' My mother dragged us outside and called 9-1-1. I wanted to go back in and use the fire extinguisher, but she wouldn't let me. She said kitchens could be replaced. Children couldn't. So I stayed outside, watching the flames grow and the smoke billow out."

"What happened to the house?" Dani asked.

"The kitchen had to be gutted and redone. The rest of the house had some smoke damage, but was okay." He smiled. "As soon as the damage was repaired, my mother had our cook fill the freezer with bags of frozen French fries. Sometimes, my mother still brings me a bag when she comes over."

"That's cute."

"Try embarrassing."

"That, too." She smiled. "But now that I know about your cooking abilities, do you mind if we make the bonbons at your place? Just in case there's another fire. I don't have renter's insurance at my apartment."

Dani winked.

"Very funny. And smart." Bryce laughed. "I don't mind at all."

He'd be willing to give a soufflé or a crème brûlée a try if it meant spending more time with Dani. He hadn't enjoyed being with a woman this much in years. Yes, he dated, but only casually. He didn't have time for anything more. Besides, finding a woman intriguing enough to put his work second probably wasn't going to happen.

"So where do you live?" she asked.

"Not too far away."

Bryce saw the expectant look in her eyes, but he preferred keeping his personal life private and didn't open up to just anyone. Except…he realized he hadn't been as guarded with Dani for some reason. Still, he wasn't ready to tell her his house in one of the more "exclusive" neighborhoods in San Francisco had been a gift. Each Delaney received a house when they graduated college. A family tradition.

He'd thought about donating the house to charity, but practicality had overcome his objections. So he'd taken the house and rented it, donating the profits to a local charity, until he'd tired of apartment living this spring and decided to move in himself. "I used to live in Cow Hollow, but recently moved to Presidio Heights."

If the neighborhood surprised her, Dani didn't show it, but she glanced at the row of elegant, pristine houses on the opposite side of the street. Mentally comparing the Marina to Presidio Heights, he wondered.

"That's a lovely neighborhood," she said. "There's a great consignment shop on Sacramento and I love that old theater, too. Not that I get to too many movies these days."

"What about you? Where do you live?"

"Inner Sunset," she said. "Not as trendy as around here, but there are some great places to eat and it's easy to get where I need to go taking public transportation."

"Except when you run into a band of menacing mimes."

Her smile lit up her face. "Except then."

She had a pretty smile. Pretty face. Pretty everything.

"Before I forget." She reached into her large bag and pulled out his jacket, neatly rolled. "Thanks for letting me borrow your coat the other night and saving me from a cold walk home from the bus stop."

"Anytime." Bryce glanced at the sun, sinking toward the horizon. Soon it would be dark and the temperature cooler. Almost time to say goodbye. Or maybe not.

"It's not that late. How does seeing a movie tonight sound?" he asked. "I can use my Black-Berry to see what's playing."

Her brows drew together, making it appear as if she were considering the offer. Good. That was better than a straight-out no.

"Okay." She placed the remaining candies into a

yellow insulated lunch box. "We can sneak what's left of the bonbons into the theater and finish them off during the movie."

"Bringing outside food in is usually against theater rules."

"Do you always follow the rules?" she asked.

"I don't suppose you do," he countered.

"Not always."

He appreciated honesty, but her answer only brought the suspicions he'd pushed to the back of his mind front and center. Instead of trying to flush out the truth, he'd spent the evening flirting and having fun.

What was going on?

Bryce never lost sight of where he was going, what he was supposed to be doing. He had never allowed his personal life to interfere with work.

Until now.

The line between investigating her and dating her was blurring to the point of being unrecognizable. He'd never met a woman who made him want to forget everything except her.

Bryce had no idea if Dani was being honest with him or not. Yet he hadn't cared. Being around her made him feel good. He liked feeling that way. Still, he couldn't forget he didn't have time for a girl-friend. He didn't want to lead Dani on. Though she might be the one leading him on.

Face it. Something out of the ordinary was going on. Here she was, dressed nicely and showing off her real looks like tonight was a real date. Not one where she'd dressed down, acting suspicious, like on their first meeting. Why the difference? Maybe it was time to say goodbye.

"If you're tired or would rather not go…" he offered.

"I want to go, but on one condition."

A condition would give him an out. A way to get some much-needed distance from her. He interacted daily with women at work, but not with this kind of relaxed interaction and flirting going on.

The switch in her from the other day bugged him. He didn't get it. Was the change because of what had happened with Gymguy and she now knew she could trust Bryce? Or the elusive something else?

"What's the condition?" Bryce asked.

"I pay for the movie."

That wasn't what he'd expected to hear. He stretched out his legs in front of him.

Having her pay for breakfast the other day had been an anomaly. Women, especially those who recognized the Delaney name, assumed he would pick up the tab and never offered to pay. Of course, Dani didn't know his last name. "I'm the one who asked you out."

"So?" She stared down her nose at him. "You

picked up dinner. I get the movie. What's the big deal?"

"Not a big deal." He wasn't old-fashioned or chauvinistic, but he had more money than he knew what to do with. Based on what she'd said so far, her taking the bus and shopping at a consignment shop, Bryce guessed she didn't have a lot of money. He didn't want her spending what little she had on him. Especially given the circumstances. Like it or not, he had to get to the bottom of what she was doing on his Web site. "But what if I want popcorn? And a soda?"

"No problem." Amusement danced in her eyes. "Feel free to order a box of candy, too."

After her bonbons? He better say no.

"Are you always so—?"

"Difficult?" she offered.

"Easy."

Her eyebrows shot up. "Excuse me?"

"Not easy as in sex. But in dating." The way her eyes narrowed told Bryce he was digging his own grave here. "Easy as in making things more equal."

She tilted her chin. "Why should one person have to foot the bill every time because past generations did it that way? Having things, especially finances, so lopsided doesn't bode well if a couple ever wants to have an equal partnership in the future."

"That's smart thinking."

"I wish I could take credit for it, but I found it on the Web site."

"Web site?" he asked.

"Blinddatebrides.com. The site has good advice on how to have a successful relationship."

Bryce's team put up new content all the time, but he'd been so busy putting out fires and thinking about Dani this week he hadn't read any of the new additions to the site. "Sounds like you've been studying up on the subject."

"Not really, since I'm not in the market for a serious relationship."

Ouch. He wasn't looking for any kind of commitment, either, but the way she dismissed one with him so easily stung. Dani might not know who he was, but several women considered him a catch.

"My friend Marissa e-mailed me the link a couple of days ago."

His suspicions shot up like a radio antenna.

Had Dani mentioned him to her online friends? Maybe they'd provided that link to help her plot how to snag a guy. That might explain why she was on the site and had started dating after so many months. And wanted to continue their date at the movies.

"Did the article say what to do if a man wouldn't let you pay?" he asked.

"Drop him like a hot potato because a man like that probably has control issues," she teased.

He didn't consider himself a control freak. "Or an unlimited supply of money," Bryce offered.

"Even the richest man in the world probably would like to be treated to a meal or movie sometime." She stared up at him, her eyes full of warmth and anticipation. "So will you let me pay for the movie?"

The hopeful tone shot straight to his heart and doused some of his suspicions. Okay, maybe she wasn't on a husband hunt. Dani might be self-reliant, tough and evasive, but at this moment she wore her emotions for the world to see. He liked seeing this side of her. "I'd be honored."

She placed the yellow insulated lunch box into her bag. "The theater will never know they are here."

But Bryce knew.

And that made him wonder...

What were the other rules that Dani didn't mind breaking?

# CHAPTER SIX

Blinddatebrides.com is running sixteen chat rooms, sixty-three private IM conferences, and 5134 members are online. Chat with your dating prospects now!

Private IM conference #59 (3 participants)…

Englishcrumpet: What happened next?

Kangagirl: Don't leave us in suspense.

DANI sat on her bed, placed her glass on the nightstand and caught up on the messages she'd missed.

Her friends cracked her up. They had been waiting for her to log on when she got home from her date and tell them all the details. She could imagine the silly grin on Marissa's face, too.

Not that Dani minded. She'd been as curious about their dating lives. She remembered the first time Marissa wrote about her temporary boss Rick, even though she'd been dating men she'd met through Blinddatebrides.com at the time. And Dani would never forget Grace's panic before her first date with Noah that her nineteen-year-old daughter Daisy had set up.

Funny how the three of them had grown closer since then, even though they'd never met in person, but Dani really wished they could. She couldn't afford to go anywhere. So far neither Marissa, with her upcoming wedding, or Grace, with her pregnancy, had time to fly to San Francisco. Maybe someday.

Sanfrandani: Sorry, I was getting a glass of water.

Kangagirl: I thought you lost your connection.

Sanfrandani: Nope, thirsty. So, the movie turned out to be one of these epic battle guy flicks. No plot. Lots of special effects and death.

Englishcrumpet: Forget the bloody movie. Tell us about you and Bryce.

Sanfrandani: LOL! I am!

Sanfrandani: The movie was so bad all we could do, other than leave, was make fun of it as we watched. Bryce has the best sense of humor. We couldn't stop laughing. People must have thought we were drunk or something.

Kangagirl: Were you drunk?

Sanfrandani: No, we drank wine with dinner, but we were just having fun at the theater.

Englishcrumpet: Tell us what happened next.

Kangagirl: And don't leave anything out.

Dani imagined her two friends, oceans away, with their gazes glued to their monitors, waiting for her to finish telling them about the date. She knew what they wanted to hear—details describing a romantic evening for two, complete with tender gazes and passionate kisses. Too bad nothing like that had happened.

Sanfrandani: The rest of the evening was pretty uneventful. He drove me home, walked me to the door and said goodnight.
Englishcrumpet: Did he kiss you?
Sanfrandani: No.
Kangagirl: Did you kiss him?
Sanfrandani: No.

As she stared at the "no" on her screen, regret and disappointment gnawed at her. She knew better than to have expectations for a not-a-real-date, but still… Dani wasn't used to a guy not staring at her body or trying to steal a kiss. Especially when she wanted him to kiss her.

Sanfrandani: There was the almost kiss during the movie, but that's it.
Kangagirl: You didn't mention an almost kiss. What happened there?

Sanfrandani: Oh, sorry. It's almost one in the morning here. Past my bedtime.

Englishcrumpet: We can wait to hear the rest if you're tired.

Sanfrandani: I'm not sure I could sleep right now.

Kangagirl: Good, because I'd rather not wait!

Sanfrandani: Well, we were sharing a bag of popcorn. Bryce leaned over to whisper something. We both reached into the bag at the same time, and our hands touched. Really our fingers. They sort of intertwined. I looked at him. His face was so close to mine. He was staring at me.

Kangagirl: Sounds romantic.

Englishcrumpet: Very.

Sanfrandani: It was the perfect moment for a kiss. Even the music soundtrack was right for it. My heart was pounding. I wanted to kiss him, but then I turned my face away.

Englishcrumpet: Why?

Sanfrandani: I didn't feel right, kissing him without him knowing the truth about me.

Kangagirl: This is serious.

Englishcrumpet: No kidding. You must really like him or you wouldn't have worried about what he would think if he found out the truth.

Kangagirl: Did you make plans to get together again?

Sanfrandani: We didn't, but…

Englishcrumpet: You like him.

Sanfrandani: More than I thought I would. But we only just met so I'm not sure why I feel this way. I mean he's gorgeous and all that, but still it's a bit disconcerting.

Kangagirl: Been there, done that.

Englishcrumpet: Welcome to the club!

Sanfrandani: I said LIKE not LOVE.

Kangagirl: We know.

Sanfrandani: I just wish I could be honest with him.

Kangagirl: If that's what you want to do, then tell him the truth.

Englishcrumpet: He's going to find out at some point if you keep seeing him.

But Dani didn't know if she should keep seeing him. Being honest with Bryce could jeopardize her job. She couldn't afford to be without a paycheck or she would have quit. She'd already wasted over six months of her life at Hookamate.com.

Kangagirl: If you're not sure what to do, then wait. You'll know when the time is right.

Dani hoped so.

But, after hearing what Bryce had to say about

where she worked, she wasn't sure he'd understand anything she had to say. And that realization tied her insides up into a knotted jumble.

Englishcrumpet: Think about what you might want to do, Dani. After all, what do you really have to lose?

My job. My heart.

Dani wasn't sure which she wanted to keep safer. Both were at stake and that scared her. Maybe it would be better if she never saw Bryce again.

She thought about his green eyes and his beautiful smile that warmed her heart.

Maybe not.

On Saturday morning, Bryce crawled out of bed. A sleepless night left him longing for extra shut-eye, but he couldn't fall back to sleep. Caitlin wanted to meet him for brunch in an hour, but he wasn't that hungry.

Not exactly true.

He wanted something. Someone. Dani.

Why hadn't he kissed her last night?

He'd had plenty of opportunity, but he'd been trying to be a gentleman. To make up for her experience with other men. Bryce had wanted her to feel safe and comfortable with him, but he needed to remember that a gentleman still kissed his date good-night.

Bryce walked to the French doors leading to a balcony and looked down at his yard.

Below, a hummingbird hovered near a blooming bougainvillea. The rapid wing motion and the way the bird flitted from one flower to the next, feeding off nectar, reminded him of Dani. Even though she'd sat with him during the picnic and at the movie, she never seemed to slow down or relax or simply be in the moment.

Was that her personality or nervousness or perhaps her age? She was only twenty-six. Six years younger than him.

He wanted the chance to find out which.

The hummingbird flew off in search of another flower. Bryce wasn't about to let Dani get away so easily. He went downstairs to his computer and typed an e-mail.

To: "Sanfrandani" <sanfrandani@blinddate-brides.com>
From: "Bigbrother" <bigbrother@blinddate-brides.com>
Subject: Today?
Had a great time last night. Any chance you are free for lunch today?

To: "Bigbrother" <bigbrother@blinddate-brides.com>
From: "Sanfrandani" <sanfrandani@blinddate-brides.com>
Subject: RE: Today?
Not unless it's a late lunch. I'm working today.


To: "Sanfrandani" <sanfrandani@blinddate-brides.com>
From: "Bigbrother" <bigbrother@blinddate-brides.com>
Subject: RE: RE: Today?
A late lunch won't work for me. I have a family thing. Tomorrow I need to check out a horse my sister is thinking of purchasing over in Danville. Want to come?


To: "Bigbrother" <bigbrother@blinddate-brides.com>
From: "Sanfrandani" <sanfrandani@blinddate-brides.com>
Subject: Yes!
I love horses. I need to finish up a project at work tomorrow, but can be done by one if that works for you.


To: "Sanfrandani" <sanfrandani@blinddate-brides.com>

From: "Bigbrother" <bigbrother@blinddate-brides.com>
Subject: RE: Yes!
One o'clock works fine. Where do you want me to pick you up?


To: "Bigbrother" <bigbrother@blinddate-brides.com>
From: "Sanfrandani" <sanfrandani@blinddate-brides.com>
Subject: RE: RE: Yes!
Pick me up at the corner of Howard and Beale. Near Starbucks. If you're running late just give me a call 555-2328. See you tomorrow :-)


Yes! A date and a phone number.

Bryce reread Dani's replies, noting the exclamation marks and the smiley face on her last e-mail. He grinned.

Many women liked flowers, others preferred chocolate, some favored sparkly jewelry.

But who would have known the way to Dani's heart was with a…horse?

"How was it?"

"The best ride of my life." Dani sat atop a gorgeous fourteen-hand bay gelding. Giddy with excitement, she smiled down at Bryce. "He's a great horse. Fabulous gait, compliant, good attitude."

"How does he handle?"

"Wonderfully. I think I'm in love." She knew Bryce had only asked her to ride the horse because she was close to Caitlin's size and hadn't ridden in months. Dani didn't care about the reasons. She leaned forward in the saddle to pat the horse's hot neck. "Did you see those lead changes? They were great."

He smiled up at her. "You were great."

She sat taller in the saddle. "Thanks. I've always felt comfortable with horses."

"It shows," he said. "You're fun to watch."

He was, too, with his dark hair gleaming in the sun and a wide smile brightening his face. "Thanks for letting me ride him."

And thank goodness she'd thought to bring her paddock boots or she might have missed the chance. What an opportunity.

With a final reluctant pat, she dismounted. She'd taken the horse through his paces and showed Bryce what he needed to know. Her job was finished.

Her feet hit the ground. She held the reins in her left hand and removed the helmet she'd borrowed from the stable with her right. "I forgot how much I enjoyed riding."

"That's what Caitlin said." Bryce took the helmet from Dani and fell in step beside her. "Her fiancé,

Mark, could tell she missed riding and told her to buy a horse. She used to be really competitive and he's encouraging her to go for it again."

As Dani led the horse around the ring to cool, she glanced toward the entrance to the indoor riding arena where the owners, a man and woman in their mid-fifties, spoke to a male rider.

Dani wiped her sweaty palms on her jeans.

The couple had kept their distance from her and Bryce once they'd realized Dani knew what she was doing. She appreciated the vote of confidence. "Caitlin will be able to do whatever she wants with this handsome fellow."

"Good to hear." Bryce moved with the grace and agility of an athlete. Dani would love to see him ride. "The vet's already done an examination. He looks like a winner. I'm going to tell Caitlin to buy him."

The horse snorted.

Dani didn't blame him one bit. She wrinkled her nose. "Is that really your job?"

"Who else's job would it be?"

"Caitlin's."

His grin crinkled the corner of his eyes. "That's one of the things I admire about you, Dani. You say exactly what's on your mind."

"If I didn't, you wouldn't know what I was thinking."

"It works both ways," Bryce said. "So you know, I'm not trying to make Caitlin's decision for her. She asked me to come out here and give my opinion. That's all. There's also something you don't know about my sister. Something you should know."

His eyes darkened.

"What?"

Bryce paused. His lips thinned into a narrow line. His serious expression worried Dani. "What is it?"

He took a deep breath. "Caitlin fell in love with a man who wasn't what he claimed to be. He stole her money and broke her heart. I don't want her to be hurt like that again so I look out for her, whether it's with love or horses."

Dani respected how he looked after his sister, yet… "That's admirable, but what about your father? Isn't he the one who's supposed to do that?"

"My father's into his own thing. He was never around much when he and my mother were married and it's gotten worse over the years." Bryce's jaw thrust forward. "He spends his time seeking young wives."

"How young?"

Bryce grimaced. "His current girlfriend is the same age as Caitlin. He's not exactly big on being a parent these days."

He acted nonchalant about the whole thing, but

an edge of bitterness in Bryce's voice made her want to reach out to him.

The horse butted her with his nose.

Okay, she could take a hint.

Dani touched Bryce's arm. His muscles rippled under her hand.

"At least your dad's still around. That counts for a lot. He could have just…"

Bryce's brows slanted. "What?"

She pulled her arm away from him. "Left."

As she led the horse toward the gate, Bryce followed.

"My dad took off when I was six," she explained. "My youngest sister was only a couple of months old. He said he loved us and would be back, but we never heard from or saw him again."

Bryce's eyes clouded with sympathy. "I'm sorry."

She didn't want his pity. "Thanks, but my mom said he wasn't cut out to be a husband and father and we're better off without him."

"You must miss him."

Dani shrugged. "I don't remember him. I have some of his DNA and his last name. That's all I ever want from him. I think what I miss is the idea of having a dad, but my sisters and I have done great, thanks to my mom."

Bryce shook his head. "I don't see how a man could desert his family like that."

Neither did she. Especially since her father had left them with nothing. But Dani wasn't about to let his selfish actions years ago ruin this beautiful day. She looked up at Bryce, the sun warming her already heated face. "Not all men are like you."

"Me?"

"Yes, you." A welcome breeze blew through her sweaty hair. "I can tell when you get married you'll be a great husband and father because of the things you do for your sister."

"I can't help being protective over the things I care about."

Would he ever care about her? Dani wasn't sure she wanted to know the answer.

As she led the horse out of the ring, his hooves kicked up dirt.

"Being protective is an honorable trait, but not many guys would spend a weekend afternoon driving to the other side of the Bay and checking out a horse their sister wanted to buy."

"Well, spending twenty-two thousand dollars on an animal deserves some checking into."

Dani stumbled. She clutched the reins. "Twenty-two—"

The price was so ridiculous she couldn't even say the amount.

Bryce nodded. "Caitlin thinks he's worth it."

Of course, she would. Dani had cleaned the stalls

and exercised horses for rich little girls like Caitlin. "The question is, do you think the horse is worth it?"

"Now that I've seen you ride him, yes."

The words came out strong and sure. His certainty made her feel good about her riding abilities, but she was having trouble coming to terms with the cost.

"Doesn't that price seem a tad…" she searched for the right word—*indulgent* and *ridiculous* probably wouldn't go down well "…excessive?"

He shrugged. "It is expensive for a horse, but you get what you pay for."

"Twenty-two thousand would pay for a lot."

Her mother didn't make that much money after taxes in a year.

A teenaged boy wearing jeans, a long-sleeved shirt and paddock boots approached them. "I'll take him from you."

Dani stared at the kid with acne on his face and a love of horses shining in his eyes. She'd been like him, mucking stalls so she could be around the animals she loved and exercise them when their owners didn't have as much time.

Bryce stood waiting, hands in his pockets.

Giving the kid the horse felt wrong though, until she remembered that was his job. Dani didn't want to get him into trouble. She handed over the reins. "I put him through his paces."

The teenager smiled. "I'll take care of him."

"Thank you." Dani watched him lead the horse away. She noticed his boots. A lot like hers. Scuffed and creased after years of use. She never could afford new ones so kept cleaning the leather with Murphy's Oil and Saddle Soap. Bryce's boots were the opposite of hers—newer and very expensive.

Uneasiness crept down her spine.

Dani knew she and Bryce were from totally different worlds, but being out here with him drove the point home. He was a horse owner; she was a stable hand.

She'd spent her high school years surrounded by people who'd treated their animals with more respect than they'd treated her. She'd lived in apartments, a car and a single-wide trailer.

He'd grown up in a world of nannies and chefs and chauffeurs. Where his father dated women young enough to be his daughter. Where paying an obscene amount for a horse was considered normal.

Her heart twisted.

"Thanks for helping me out today," he said.

"It was my pleasure."

And it was. In spite of the jolt of reality, she'd enjoyed being with him today. Truth be told, she didn't want the day to end. She didn't want their differences to come between them. She wanted to focus on the good things, not what gave her pause.

For the first time in a long while, Dani wanted

to believe in happy endings, that obstacles, no matter how big, could be overcome. That just because people came from opposite worlds, things could still work out. That loving someone didn't mean you'd eventually be left with nothing but a broken heart.

"Being out here has been like a dream come true," she admitted.

"I know." The intensity of his eyes made her feel as if she were the only woman in the world. "I wouldn't want to be here with anyone but you."

Her breath caught in her throat. Dani wanted to be the only one for him. She forced herself to breathe.

Dani didn't want to care. A lifetime of being disappointed, of struggling, of simply surviving didn't want her to care. But, heaven help her, she did care. About what he'd said. About him. She couldn't help herself.

"Me, either," she said.

Desire flared in Bryce's eyes, but his attention didn't make her feel cheap, like some man's possession or plaything *du jour.* He made her feel beautiful, sexy, wanted. A way she hadn't felt in…forever.

She wanted him to kiss her. Her lips parted in hope.

He lowered his head and covered her mouth with his. The touch of his lips brought a jolt of electricity crackling through her.

His lips ran over hers with such tenderness tears stung Dani's eyes. His kiss flowed through her, a current of affection, filling all the empty spaces inside with warmth.

He tasted like the coffee they'd drunk on the drive—warm, strong and rich. But there was more—salt, heat, male.

She drank up his kiss as if she'd never taste another drop.

As he increased the pressure of his mouth, her knees went weak. She'd heard the phrase "being kissed senseless." She finally understood what those words meant.

She wrapped her arms around his shoulders to keep from falling.

If he kept kissing her this way, she'd be a puddle on the ground.

Dani didn't think she would mind.

The familiar scents of dirt, hay and horse reminded her of the farm, but here in Bryce's kiss she'd found the only home she needed.

His arms wrapped around her, pulling her against his chest. Dani wanted to get closer. Body pressed against body. She hadn't realized he was so strong, so solid before.

All the while his lips caressed, his tongue explored.

Sensation pulsated through her. She hadn't known it was possible to feel this way.

Every nerve ending sizzled. Her stomach quivered. Her heart melted.

This was how she'd dreamed of being kissed someday. Dani couldn't believe it was happening now. Here. With Bryce.

She might not have been looking for a boyfriend, but somehow she'd found him. And, even though she didn't want a relationship, she might need one.

The realization should have scared her more than it did.

As Dani ran her hands through his hair, he trailed kisses along her jawline. She arched back, wanting…

More.

He returned to her mouth, stealing her breath and her heart…

Warning bells sounded. Rational thought returned. With her hands on his shoulders, she pulled her lips away from his.

The emotion in his eyes and the smile on his face made her want to start kissing him all over again.

But that would be too dangerous. She didn't want to lose herself in him. She couldn't.

Dani tried to catch her breath, regain control.

He pushed a strand of her hair off her face. "That was amazing."

Awesome was more like it. She stared up at him, wanting to memorize everything about him, from the faint lines at the corner of his eyes to the way he smoothed her hair with his hand. "Yes, amazing."

Somewhere a horse neighed.

"Ready to head back to the city?" Bryce asked.

No. A sense of inadequacy swept over her. She wanted to go somewhere else—a neutral place, where they could just be themselves and not have to worry about their jobs, their families, their lives. Their differences.

"Not really," she admitted.

Bryce laced his fingers with hers and gave a squeeze. "We can come back."

*We.*

Hope surged. Dani didn't want to let go. She didn't want to say goodbye.

Not today. Not ever.

She looked up at him. The tenderness in his expression brought a sigh to her lips.

Happiness bubbled, threatening to spill from her heart. She wanted this feeling to last.

Today, tomorrow, always.

That couldn't happen unless she did one thing…

Tell Bryce the truth.

About her job. About everything.

# CHAPTER SEVEN

"WOULD you like something to drink?" Standing in the doorway to her kitchen, Dani wrung her hands. "Eat?"

Bryce wanted to put her at ease, not make her wait on him. "No, thanks."

Her nervousness disturbed him. Especially after the great time they'd had at the stable.

He understood how she felt though. They were alone in her studio apartment after some really hot kisses. He was a bit on edge himself. Maybe a little conversation would help.

"Nice place." Bryce noticed the futon sofa that probably doubled as her bed. He looked away. "Comfortable."

"Thanks." Her voice sounded shaky. "It's small, but I don't need a lot of space."

A photograph of her riding a large black horse caught his attention. Even in the still frame, he could see the fluidity of her body as she and the animal made a jump. "Where was this picture taken?"

Her faint smile seemed to relax the rest of her face. "A stable near the farm where I worked during high school."

He noticed she was wearing the same old paddock boots in the photo as she'd worn today. Functional and well-worn. She deserved new ones. "You should come out to my family's stable and ride."

Uncertainty crept into her eyes. "You have a stable?"

Darn, he'd wanted to put a smile on her pretty face, not make her feel worse. "Not me, my family."

She paced in front of the doorway to the kitchen. She reminded him, not of a humming-bird, intent on reaching its next destination, but of a cat, trying to decide whether to chase after a mouse or not. The indecision seemed out of character for Dani.

Something must be on her mind. Bryce hoped she wasn't thinking he wanted to take their kiss further. Okay, he did, but not if it made her act like this. He wished he could go back and change things because, even though he liked Dani, he didn't like the complications relationships often brought with them.

Not that kissing her meant he was in a relationship. Yet…she'd gotten under his skin.

Her friendliness, her sense of humor, even her evasiveness intrigued him. And he couldn't deny he wanted to kiss her again.

Bryce crossed the room and held her hands. "Today has been great, but since we got here you seem a little tense. Don't be. There's no rush. The only thing I want is to see you smile."

"I want to smile, except…"

He led her over to the futon and pulled her down so she was seated next to him. He kept hold of her hand. "Tell me what's going on."

She took a breath. And another. "Well, you know I've told you how I grew up."

Bryce nodded. "You didn't have it easy. No father. No place to live at times."

"We're very different."

She'd mentioned that before. Maybe he could ease her concerns. "In some ways, we are. No matter whether someone's family has money or not, I believe a person has to make their own way in life. I've done that. And so have you. I respect how much you've overcome, Dani. I just wish you didn't have it so tough, but look at the person you are now. Where you are. That's what counts."

Dani looked at the floor. "I'm not very happy with where I am now. I mean I'm happy I'm with you, but not…my job situation."

The sadness in her voice squeezed his heart. He'd been wrong about what she was worried about. He rubbed her hand with his thumb.

"When I graduated with an MBA, I thought I'd

finally made it. Put the past behind me." She got a faraway look in her eyes. "I was sure I had everything I needed. A dream job, a cool apartment, a new car, enough money to more than cover my expenses, student loans and still be able to help my family out each month and then…

"I was laid off from my marketing position at Clickznos at the beginning of the year."

"One of the buyout casualties."

She nodded.

He squeezed her hand.

"I'd recently been promoted and gotten a big raise." Her voice sounded almost wistful. "I suppose the signals were there, but we were working too hard to notice them. We assumed things were okay, that we'd be taken care of, but all but a handful of us soon found ourselves on the street with a 'thanks for your hard work' goodbye and a pitiful, almost insulting severance package."

He placed his arm around her. "That had to be tough."

She nodded. "I had a savings account, but I also help my youngest sister pay for college and my mother with her medical insurance so the money didn't last long. I had college and grad school loans to pay for. Bills started piling up fast. I did what I could while I searched for a comparable job. I downsized and moved into this place. I sold my car.

But I couldn't wait any longer for the perfect position to materialize. I needed a paycheck so I took a job that under normal circumstances I would have never considered."

Her worried eyes watched him. Waiting.

So this was what she'd been keeping from him. Relief flooded him. That explained why she didn't mind him not discussing his work. She hadn't wanted to discuss hers either.

He remembered what he'd checked on her profile. "You're in sales?"

"Kind of…sort of…but not really." She blew out a puff of air. "It's complicated."

"Life is complicated," he said. "We can work through anything if you believe we can."

A beat passed. A clock ticked.

"I have a job." She cleared her throat. "It's just not a job I'm particularly proud of."

"Nothing wrong with flipping burgers."

"Except when it doesn't pay."

He stared at her. "Then what…"

She stared at her lap.

Lap dancer? Okay, that was a leap from fast food, but she had the looks and the body. Plus the money was good.

Bryce smiled. Not exactly the job he'd imagined his girlfriend doing, but he wasn't about to judge her, especially under these circumstances. "You found a job that worked at the time. I could never hold what you do against you."

"Sure?"

"You're more than your job, Dani. More than what's on the outside. I like your tenacity, your character. I care for you."

Relief filled her eyes. The tightness disappeared from around her mouth. "I really needed to hear you say that."

He kissed the top of her hand. "So what do you do?"

She straightened and took another breath. "I'm marketing director for Hookamate.com."

Bryce flinched. He let go of her hand as if it were a grenade with a missing pin.

Lines creased her forehead. "Bryce…"

He looked away, trying to come to terms with what he'd just heard.

*I'm a spy.*

Hookamate.com.

Everything clicked into place.

He swallowed. "I don't believe this."

Her gaze implored him. "You said my job didn't matter."

"That was when I thought you might be a stripper."

She stiffened. "A stripper?"

"Or lap dancer."

"That's so insulting." Her chin jutted forward. "I really thought you were different from other guys, but you aren't. You think I can only use my body to make a living, not my brain."

"You really think James Richardson hired you to be one of his lackeys because of your IQ?"

Her mouth tightened. "I've made a difference at Hookamate.com."

"Oh, yeah, I'd be real proud of the results of your spying on me."

"You?"

Bryce ignored the confusion in Dani's eyes. He pretended not to see her lower lip tremble. He focused on all the problems Blinddatebrides.com had been having with scammers. Problems he should have been investigating instead of wasting his time with her. "I used to work with the guy. He's had some sort of vendetta against me since I left."

"You worked with him, so that means you're…?"

"Bryce Delaney."

Her face paled. "The founder and CEO of Blinddatebrides.com."

He nodded once.

She slumped against the futon. The hurt in her eyes told him that she'd had no idea who he was. At least she hadn't been using him to get information. The realization didn't make him feel any less betrayed.

"You knew about me this entire time." Disbelief and anger dripped from each word.

"I didn't know why you were on the site, but a

chat filter picked up the words *I'm a spy*." He kept his voice cool, calm. "We've been trying to figure out what that meant ever since."

"We?"

"My security team and me."

She winced. "So all of…um…our dates…"

"An investigation."

Who was the one who was lying now? Bryce didn't care.

Dani bit her lip. "So while I was spying on Blinddatebrides.com, you were spying on me."

"Investigating you," he countered.

"Without my knowledge."

"Yes."

She sat only two feet away from him, but the space felt insurmountable. He liked her. Or had liked her. He wasn't sure what he felt now.

She glared at him. "Guess that gives new meaning to your user name."

"Don't put this on me." He stood, not wanting to be drawn into an argument. "You're the one who broke the terms of service. Everyone's wondered why Hookamate.com's traffic ranking has been up for the past four months. Now I know the answer. Were you there to steal content or was hacking and sabotaging the site part of your job description, too?"

"None of the above." She rose and walked to the

opposite side of the room. "I gave James screen shots, but I never stole anything. I used the site to get ideas and create new content for ours. Traffic is up because I was doing my job. And a damn good job at that."

She placed her hands on her hips. "And I never did anything else on your site. No hacking. No sabotage. I might have broken your TOS, but I followed every other rule, especially when another user contacted me. That's why I turned down dates. It wasn't fair to lead them on when I had no interest in dating."

"I find it very hard to believe you." His words sounded harsh to his own ears. Suddenly, he didn't care about remaining in control. "What did you say that night after your date with Gymguy? 'Players and liars are everywhere.' Guess you spoke from experience."

"You, too." She drew her lips into a thin line. "You admitted following Hookamate's traffic rankings. Every company checks out their competitors. It's irresponsible not to. Yes, I crossed the line when I joined the site, but I was only doing my job."

"Your job?" Bryce's temper flared. "Joining a community, making friends, going on dates so you could spy. Having men fall…"

Damn her. He'd known about the red flags, yet he'd wanted to believe she was on the level.

So much for taking care of his Web site, customers and company. He was no smarter than those suckers who got conned out of their hard-earned money by responding to foreign spammers' e-mails asking for money to be wired overseas.

Still curiosity got the better of him. "Why did you go out with me?"

"James wanted me to put together a clientele profile and see what clients really thought of Blind-datebrides.com. I only went out with you and Gymguy. No one else contacted me after that."

"I turned off your participation in the compatibility matching program and site search engine."

"Why?"

"The investigation," Bryce admitted. "I wanted to make sure you weren't a troublemaker and trying to cause problems with clients."

She pursed her lips. "You didn't want me going out with any other guys."

A beat passed, and another. "Maybe not."

Definitely not. And, from the expression on her face, she knew it.

"That night at the restaurant. You knew I'd be there with Gymguy."

Bryce nodded once.

"How?" she asked.

"Your e-mail."

"And you're upset over what I was doing?" Her

eyes darkened to a midnight-blue. "Reading e-mail is an invasion of privacy. It's—"

"Part of the terms of service you agreed to when you signed onto Blinddatebrides.com."

"It's still not right," she said. "We've both been keeping secrets but, except for telling you about my job and why I joined the site, I was open and honest about everything. I never lied to you or invaded your privacy."

"I was doing my job."

"And, as I said, I was doing mine," she countered. "I had misgivings over doing it, but it's still part of doing business on the Internet. I'm sure there are other competitors who signed up at Blinddatebrides.com, too."

But he hadn't just kissed them passionately or wanted to kiss them again. "If I find out about them, I'll kick them off. I want Blinddatebrides.com to be a safe place."

"Safe doesn't exist, Bryce. You just proved that to me by saying my job didn't matter when it does. At least I was honest about my feelings for you, unlike you."

"I've been honest."

"If that's your version of honesty, I'd hate to see you being dishonest." She pressed her lips together. "I'll admit what I did wasn't right, but neither was what you just did to me.

"And, just so you know, I didn't want to join your site or go on dates, but James threatened to fire me if I didn't. I couldn't afford to quit."

"You've thought about quitting?" Bryce asked.

"Every single day since I signed up for an account on Blinddatebrides.com over six months ago."

The sincerity in her voice clawed at his heart. Everything he believed people capable of—misrepresenting themselves and lying—was right here in the room. He was guilty of it himself which made this all the more confusing.

He didn't know what to say or do.

Everything they'd experienced, everything they could share together in the future, was unraveling. The way they were arguing reminded him of his parents fighting. A part of him wanted to walk away and not look back. Yet another part couldn't imagine never seeing her again. Never kissing her.

Blood pounded at his temples. A headache threatened to erupt. He squeezed his eyes shut.

When he opened them, she was staring at him.

"I never wanted to hurt anyone. That's why I wrote the profile I did. So guys wouldn't want to go out with me. I'm sorry if I hurt you. That wasn't my intention." Her eyes glistened. "I'll cancel my account tonight."

Bryce hated feeling the way he did, but he also hated seeing Dani so upset. "What about your friends?"

"We know each other's personal e-mail addresses. There are other places on the Internet where we can chat and send IMs from."

"What about your job?"

The truth was clear in her eyes. She expected to be fired. "Why do you care?"

He shouldn't care. "Because you told me what drove you to take the job in the first place. I'm not the bad guy here."

"No, you're just the hypocrite telling me one thing and doing another. I trusted you. I believed what you said. But you used my falling for you to set a trap."

She'd fallen for him? Bryce wasn't sure what to think or believe right now.

"I just wonder what your reaction would have been if I'd been a stripper. I doubt you'd have been so understanding then, either."

Her criticism stung. The disapproval in her voice made him feel like a jerk. "Don't cancel your account until you find another job."

Her shoulders sagged for a moment, then she straightened. "I've been trying to find a job for months with no luck so that might take a while."

"As long as you work for James, you can use my site for e-mailing and chatting with your two friends. Nothing else."

"Will you be checking up on me?"

Bryce's jaw clenched. "What do you think?"

Blinddatebrides.com is running sixteen chat rooms, forty-seven private IM conferences, and 7305 members are online. Chat with your dating prospects now!

Private IM conference #28 (3 participants)…

**Sanfrandani:** I feel so bad.

**Englishcrumpet:** Don't worry, Dani. We can find another place to chat if we need to. The main thing is we don't lose touch.

**Sanfrandani:** I agree. At least he didn't kick me off the site right away, but I'm sure that's coming.

**Kangagirl:** Have you heard anything from Bryce?

Anger surged. Granted, Dani was the one who'd joined the Web site under false pretenses, but Bryce had had no reason to set her up so she'd spill her soul to him and then have him turn on her the way he had.

Whatever they'd shared before no longer existed. She wondered if a connection ever had.

**Sanfrandani:** Nope. It's been a week.

At least she'd apologized for her part in the mess. Telling her she could stay on the site didn't count as an apology in her book.

Englishcrumpet: What about your job search?
Sanfrandani: Still nothing. It's like my résumé disappears into a black hole every time I send one out. It's really frustrating. James keeps asking about my dates. I've been putting him off, but I'm going to have to say something to him soon.
Englishcrumpet: A job will turn up.
Kangagirl: Fingers crossed.
Englishcrumpet: Are you going to contact Bryce?
Sanfrandani: There's no need. We're over.
Englishcrumpet: I'm sorry.
Kangagirl: Me, too. I know you liked him.
Sanfrandani: Thanks, but I'm more angry than sad. I'll survive.

And she would.

She'd just wanted to believe there was a man out there she could trust and love. She'd wanted that man to be Bryce.

"Check this out."

In his office, Bryce turned the monitor on his desk so his coworkers could see what he'd spent his days and nights working on this week. He'd needed something to focus his attention on so he wouldn't think about…

Dani.

Grant stared at the HTML page displayed on the monitor. His smile widened. "That is one sweet honeypot."

"Where?" Peering over Grant's shoulder, Joelle adjusted her plastic-rimmed glasses. "I don't see anything except code."

Grant continued reading the screen. "That's because you're a non-techie, Joelle."

"A non-techie who makes sure you receive a paycheck."

"Look right here." Bryce highlighted lines of commented-out code that gave clues of how the internals of the site were implemented. "When a hacker tries to exploit the code he's found, he'll think he's hit gold, except what he's really found is fake user info on an isolated network. We can then hunt him down. It would feel good to actually catch one of these losers trying to mess with the site."

"And if you can't catch them?" Joelle asked.

"The data we get can help mitigate our risk," Grant said.

Bryce leaned back in his chair. "I just hope someone takes the bait."

"I'm sure they will," Joelle said. "You're really good at setting traps, boss."

She'd meant the words as a compliment, but they echoed Dani's a little too closely.

*I trusted you. I believed what you said. But you used my falling for you to set a trap.*

And that was exactly what he'd done.

He'd misled Dani by saying one thing, then doing another.

The same way he'd built the honeypot into the code to catch hackers.

Dani hadn't been honest about who she was. Neither had he.

His intentions had been good. Hers hadn't.

But she'd been honest about her feelings. And he...

Bryce sighed. He owed her an apology.

The only question was, after their fight, would Dani even want to listen to one?

To: "Sanfrandani" <sanfrandani@blinddate-brides.com>
From: "Bigbrother" <bigbrother@blinddate-brides.com>
Subject: Pot. Kettle. Black.
I'm not Colonel Brandon, but I'm not Willoughby, either. I owe you an apology for setting you up the way I did. It wasn't intentional. How does meeting at Crossroads before work tomorrow to discuss sound? My treat.
-b

To: "Bigbrother" <bigbrother@blinddate-brides.com>
From: "Sanfrandani" <sanfrandani@blinddate-brides.com>
Subject: RE: Pot. Kettle. Black.
Well, no one would ever mistake me for Marianne Dashwood.
Open to discussion, but busy in the morning. Free for lunch. Anytime from 11:30 to 1:30. Let me know.
-d

To: "Sanfrandani" <sanfrandani@blinddate-brides.com>
From: "Bigbrother" <bigbrother@blinddate-brides.com>
Subject: Lunch
See you at noon. Just look for the black pot.
-b

Uncertainty filled Dani as she sat in her lonely cubicle rereading Bryce's e-mails. She stirred in her chair, unsure what meeting him would bring. Still a kernel of hope remained.

Hope that Bryce meant what he said about apologizing for his part in their fight.

Hope that he forgave her for her part in all this.

Hope that maybe he was different from other men and things between them might not be totally over.

At twelve o'clock, Dani entered the café. Lunch customers packed the place. Conversations from the crowd filled the air.

She spotted Bryce sitting at a table not far from the one they'd occupied the first time they'd met. He wore a gray suit with a white dress shirt and a yellow tie.

Dani was still angry over what had happened in her apartment, but the butterflies flapping and wreaking havoc in her stomach had nothing to do with her being upset and everything to do with attraction. He seemed to have gotten better-looking over the last week. Darn him.

A glass crashed to the floor.

An omen, perhaps? She wasn't sure whether to move forward or retreat. Maybe he hadn't seen her...

Bryce's gaze caught her. His face brightened.

Maybe he was happy to see her. Maybe he wanted to get this over with.

Dani inhaled deeply to muster her courage. She could do this. She had no choice really since she'd said she was open for discussion. Unlike him, she wasn't going to renege on her word.

He offered her a forgiving smile and raised a small black pot in the air.

She half laughed. He hadn't been kidding about the pot.

Okay, maybe she was overreacting a little. The least she could do was have lunch with him and hear what he had to say.

She wove her way to his table, taking advantage of the time to prepare herself. All she wanted from him was an apology. Not a handshake or hug or kiss…

Bryce stood. "Miss Kettle?"

"Mr. Pot, I presume?"

He nodded.

Tension simmered between them, a strong mix of anxiety and attraction. She stood across from him like a total stranger.

Dani swallowed. Agreeing to meet him was a really bad idea.

A cell phone rang somewhere near the bookshelves.

"Do you want to order lunch before we sit?" Bryce asked finally.

"Sure," Dani said, even though she didn't have much of an appetite at the moment.

She followed him to the counter, where they ordered sandwiches and drinks. Bryce paid as he'd said he would.

Back at the table, Dani sat across from him. She heard the typing of keys on a laptop. She squeezed a slice of lemon into her iced tea and stole a glance at his face.

He was staring at her.

"I'm sorry." Bryce's voice cut through the silence at their table and the noise around them. "You took responsibility for your actions. I didn't. I apologize for not being honest with you, for setting you up like that and everything else I said and did. It wasn't fair of me."

Those were the words Dani needed to hear. "Thank you. I know you feel betrayed over something very important to you. I appreciate and accept your apology."

"Good, because I don't like how things are between us."

She stirred her iced tea. "There isn't anything between us."

"But I want there to be again," he said with such heartfelt honesty she dropped her spoon. "After everything that's happened, I miss what we had. I miss you, Dani. I might have started to see you under false pretenses, but my feelings for you were never faked. The things I said on our dates, the kissing, all that was true and not part of my checking up on you."

She stared at him, transfixed by the emotion in his eyes and his voice.

"I know you said you weren't interested in dating, but I want to keep seeing you. If you're game, we could start over."

"Start over," she repeated, fighting the tumble of confused thoughts and emotions in her head.

"Yes, we could wipe the slate clean," he explained. "Knowing what we know about each other now, we put what happened behind us and start fresh. This could be our first date."

The unexpected proposition had her heart dancing a two-step, but doubts swirled. Dani wasn't about to step onto the dance floor just yet. "What about my job? I still haven't found another one."

"Did you sign a non-disclosure agreement?"

She nodded.

"What about a non-compete clause?"

Another nod.

"Then I can't offer you a job."

"Nothing personal, but I wouldn't want to work for you," she admitted. "I learned from my mother that it's best to take charge of your own life and not rely on others to give you what you need."

That was something her mother hadn't done after she married and paid the price when Dani's father left. She would not make the same mistake.

A woman with a short asymmetric haircut delivered their sandwiches and walked away.

"I understand that, but what if I send your résumés out to some people I know?" Bryce offered. "I have a lot of connections that could come in handy."

"I…" Dani knew former coworkers had found jobs through contacts. That was how most people found new positions. And she couldn't pretend her own job search had yielded anything except feelings of futility. "As long as you only give them my résumé and promise to do nothing else. I don't want something just handed to me because I know you."

"Getting the job will be up to you."

"That's what I needed to hear." Satisfied, she smiled. "Thanks."

"Are you always so independent?"

"Yes."

"E-mail your résumé when you get home tonight."

"Thanks." Except a question niggled at her. "You talked about starting over. How does that work? Do we wait until I get a new job or…"

"I don't want to wait," Bryce said without any hesitation. "I want to see you as much as I can."

"I'd like that, too," she admitted. "But we have to be honest with each other from now on. You have work and so do I. Plus I need to find a new job. Given the circumstances, we might want to take things…slow."

Bryce smiled back. "Slow works for me."

# CHAPTER EIGHT

Instant Message from Dani to Grace and Marissa: *Trying 2 work things out with Bryce. Cross ur fingers! TTYL!*

Instant Message from Grace to Dani: *Good luck! Keep us posted. But please be careful.*

Instant Message from Marissa to Dani: *Fingers crossed! Watch out for yourself, okay?*

Instant Message from Marissa to Grace: *Do you know what's going on with Dani and Bryce? I'm a little worried.*

Instant Message from Grace to Marissa: *No idea! But it sounds like we might not have to find a new place to chat!!!*

OVER the next two weeks, Bryce's work and travel schedule kept him busy. He only saw Dani twice, but kept in touch with her via phone calls, texting and e-mails. She didn't mind his work taking up so much of his time. She had things to do herself.

By the time Friday rolled around, he couldn't wait to see her. Thoughts of this evening had kept him going today, through an interview with a technology blogger, a phone call from his father and a meeting with his attorney.

Rain pelted Bryce as he ran from his car to the Palace of Fine Arts, where he was supposed to have met her twenty minutes ago.

Helluva time to be late.

The relentless storm had flooded roads, turning the city streets into gridlock with backed-up drains and fender benders.

He lengthened his stride, his feet pounding against the wet pavement. Water beaded on his jacket and dripped from his hair.

The entire park was deserted. A foghorn blared in the distance. Not the ideal conditions for a romantic picnic beneath the stars.

He should have checked the weather forecast before leaving the office. He'd tried to call Dani, but gotten her voice mail. Not that he would have canceled. Storm or not, he wanted to see her. He only hoped she hadn't gotten caught in the downpour, too.

Up ahead, lights illuminated the columns and the interior of the dome. Dani would be underneath the rotunda waiting for him. The way she had been the first time they'd been here.

Anticipation surged. Bryce accelerated.

For once they had nowhere else to go, nothing else to do but be together.

He focused on the rotunda. Almost there.

Cold water shot up his pant leg. His shoe squished against the concrete.

Damn. Bryce glanced down at a big puddle. He shook his foot and continued on. A little more water didn't matter when he was already soaking wet.

He ran underneath the dome, out of the cold rain and into the light. The first thing he saw was…

Dani.

She leaned against a column, looking like a goddess from ancient times except for the small cooler and picnic basket at her feet.

The sight warmed Bryce right up.

Water dripped from the hair plastered against her head and onto her soaking wet pale blue jacket. The thin, wet fabric clung to her like a second skin, accentuating every curve of her body and leaving little to his imagination.

Awareness rippled through him.

He wanted her.

It was as simple and as complicated as that.

"Looks like I'm not the only one who forgot an umbrella," she said.

Her wide smile sent his pulse sprinting through his veins.

"Nope." His gaze raked over her once again.

Talk about a feast for the eyes. "But I'm glad you forgot yours."

Dani raised her chin. "Why is that?"

"Because you are totally hot, Miss Bennett."

He walked toward her. She met him halfway with a wry grin on her face.

"You're not so bad yourself, Mr. Delaney."

Bryce stood across from her at the center of the dome. The darker sapphire flecks in her eyes mesmerized him. He hadn't noticed them before. "It's hard to believe we were here only a few weeks ago."

"This does have a bit of a déjà vu feeling."

"Except for the rain."

Her gaze remained locked on his. "The darkness."

"And this…"

Bryce covered her mouth with his. She tensed for a moment, then relaxed, moving her soft lips against his. He didn't know how long they stood there with only their lips touching. He didn't care.

Kissing her like this was what he'd been thinking about, dreaming about, wanting to do, ever since they'd started over. Okay, ever since the kiss at the stable. He wasn't about to rush through the opportunity. He wanted to savor the moment, make it last.

Dani's kiss, full of sweetness and warmth, like the woman herself, was addictive. Intoxicating. A mysterious elixir with a secret ingredient. Bryce wanted more.

He deepened the kiss, wrapping his arms around her.

Sheets of rain fell from the sky, drumming against the dome and the cement beyond the rotunda. The pounding water matched the beat of his heart.

His hand splayed her back, the wet fabric beneath his palm, and he pulled her toward him.

Dani went willingly, eagerly against him. She wrapped her arms around him, running the palms of her hands over his shoulders and back. A ball of need formed low in his stomach, an ache only she could soothe.

He moved his lips away from hers, trailing kisses along her jawline. She arched, giving him access to her neck. He showered kiss after kiss.

She moaned.

Heated blood pulsated through his veins. The hot ache grew inside him.

Dani wove her fingers through his hair. She rose up to kiss him, but bypassed his mouth and went straight to his ear. She nibbled on his earlobe, ran her tongue over it.

Bryce felt himself sinking into her.

He didn't care. The only thing he cared about was...

Her.

The realization jolted him. He pulled away.

She stared up at him with wide eyes filled with desire.

Bryce placed his hand on her flushed face; her normally warm skin was wet and cold. "We said we were starting over and were going slow, but I don't want to go backward, Dani."

"Me, either." She wet her lips and looked around. "I don't think we're going to be able to have much of a picnic here."

"We could have a picnic on my living room floor," he suggested, not caring where they ended up as long as they remained together. "It won't be the same as this place, but it's warm and dry."

"Sounds good."

Very good. Spending time alone at his house with a rain-soaked, sexy, intelligent woman on a dark and stormy night was as good as it got.

A satisfied smile settled on Bryce's face. "Let's make a run for my car."

Playing house as a kid had never been this fun. When Bryce had said he lived in Presidio Heights, she'd thought he meant an apartment not a multi-million-dollar house.

Dani stood in Bryce's gourmet kitchen and rolled up the sleeves of his shirt, which she was wearing. A drawer opened and closed behind her. She pulled up his sweatpants that kept slipping down her hips.

Her lips tingled from the kiss under the rotunda and her body felt cold without Bryce's arms around her.

Face it, she liked him. A lot. The realization didn't terrify her as much as it once would have. But she still needed to be smart about things and move slowly.

A pop sounded behind her—the cork from the wine bottle.

She shot a sideways glance Bryce's way. His damp hair curled at the ends. His casual clothes, a long-sleeved brown T-shirt and green trackpants, made him seem more real and less like some fantasy guy in a designer suit from a glossy magazine. And that made him appeal to her even more. Darn it.

She would have to make sure he didn't kiss her again tonight. Or she didn't kiss him. Otherwise, she might find herself wanting to rush into something with him.

Dani looked away, wrapping her hands around her.

"Your clothes should be dry soon." Bryce handed her a glass of red wine from the bottle she'd brought for their picnic. "I have a bottle of Chardonnay if you prefer."

The hunger in his gaze made her think he wasn't only interested in tasting dinner. Too bad she wouldn't mind another taste of him. Dani gulped.

No more kisses, she reminded herself.

"Thanks." She tried to sound relaxed, even though every single one of her muscles was bunched up in knots. She took a sip of the Pinot Noir. "This will go better with the dinner I made."

"Whatever you brought smells delicious."

He was delicious. Eating dinner ASAP made a whole lot of sense; otherwise she might have to taste him. Dani set her glass on the smooth granite countertop. "I'd better dish up the food before it gets too cold."

"I'll lay out the blanket in front of the fireplace in the living room," he said.

Oh, boy, that sounded romantic. Maybe they should eat here at the kitchen island and sit on stools instead.

Before she could say anything, Bryce disappeared through the butler's pantry, leaving Dani alone in the to-die-for kitchen.

She hadn't wanted a man in her life, but she seemed to have found one. A good one. If she weren't careful, she could find herself in a serious relationship. And that wasn't sounding like such a bad thing at the moment.

With a resigned sigh, she padded barefoot across the wide-planked hardwood floor.

Music played, streaming from speakers she hadn't known were there. He must have turned on a sound system. As she placed a marinated steak and vegetable kebob on each plate, a soft melody filled the kitchen.

"Do you like to dance?" Bryce asked.

Dani realized she was swaying to the music. She stopped, embarrassed. "I don't get much opportunity to dance."

Standing behind her, he placed his hands on her shoulders. "But you like dancing."

It wasn't a question. Still Dani nodded. That was the only response she could manage.

Standing with him like this felt so comfortable and right. She fought the urge to lean back against him. They seemed like a…couple. She straightened and added a scoop of rice pilaf to the plates instead. "What about you?"

"I'm not really into dancing," he admitted. "My mother forced dancing lessons on me when I was a kid."

"Let me guess." Dani placed a salad with fresh strawberries and poppy seed dressing on the plates. "You didn't like the lessons."

"I hated them." Bryce picked up his wineglass. "I'll never forget having to dance in front of all the parents. All those eyes watching me, seeing every mistake. It was a living nightmare. One I don't want to repeat."

She picked up the plates and silverware, wrapped in napkins. "Everything's ready."

He tucked the wine bottle in the nook of his arm and grabbed their glasses. She followed him into the living room.

A blanket lay on the floor in front of the roaring fire. Flickering candles on the built-in shelves and mantel added to the romantic atmosphere.

A mix of emotion welled inside her. His thoughtfulness at making things so special for their "picnic" and her worry that she might find herself caught up in the moment. She sat on the blanket. "This is lovely, Bryce. Thanks for going to so much trouble."

"You're welcome. But you deserve the thanks for going to all the trouble with a home-cooked meal." He took a plate from Dani, sat across from her and swallowed a forkful of rice pilaf. "This is fantastic. Where did you learn to cook?"

"My mother taught me." Dani removed the stick from her kebob. "She cooks at the farm and had us help her sometimes. During college, I worked at a café near campus."

"Is there anything you can't do?"

She drank her wine. "Find a job."

"You will. Your résumé is out there." He reached across the blanket and touched her hand. "Remember, finding a good job doesn't happen overnight. Give it time."

Staring into his eyes made her think everything—job, life, even love—would work out. Somehow. "Okay."

As they finished eating dinner and he explained where he'd sent her résumé, she noticed the architectural details of the living room. The moldings, the wood-paned windows, French doors. She could imagine herself in the drawing room at Netherfield.

Only Bryce was much sharper than Mr. Bingley and more amenable and approachable than Mr. Darcy. "This is a beautiful house."

"Thanks." Bryce placed his fork on his plate. "I've managed to get two rooms remodeled, but there's more to do."

"Are you going to be doing heavy construction or just surface, cosmetic stuff?" she asked.

"No wall moving," he said. "Painting, window coverings and new furniture."

She smiled. "The fun stuff."

"You might think so."

"Come on. You get to decorate your own house. That's—" she searched for the right words "—a dream come true for many people. I'd love to have a house to do that with. I remember…"

"What?" Bryce asked.

"Nothing." She stared into her wineglass, feeling self-conscious. "It's silly."

"No holding back," Bryce urged. "Please tell me what you were going to say."

"When I was younger, I used to draw floor plans for houses. There would be tons of scrap paper with my scribbles on them everywhere. One Christmas, I got a book, one of those thick magazines really, of house plans. It was my favorite present. I still have it somewhere."

"Did you want to be an architect?" he asked.

She watched the flames dancing in the fireplace. "No, I just wanted to have my own house."

"If you have any ideas for mine, I'm open to suggestions."

"Be careful," she warned. "I share my suggestions as much as my opinions."

"I don't mind." Bryce refilled her wineglass. "That will be better than my mother having interior designers call to set up appointments I don't want."

"Echoes of your dancing lessons?"

"Yep." He grinned. "She can't understand why I'm not in any hurry to get the house done right away."

"I'd think you'd want to live here a while and get a feel for the place first."

"That's exactly what I told her, but I'm not holding my breath she'll listen." He leaned back on his elbows. "My mother likes getting her way, but now that Caitlin and I are older that doesn't always happen."

"Most people prefer getting their way," Dani said. "I know I do."

"What would you like right now?" Bryce asked.

A kiss. No, that wouldn't be smart, considering the circumstances. She'd go for second best. "How about dessert?"

"This brownie is the most decadent I've ever tasted and, no doubt, going straight to my hips." Dani's pink tongue darted out and licked her lips. "These have to be homemade, but I thought you said you couldn't cook."

Busted. Bryce couldn't lie. "I never said I made them. Just that I was bringing dessert."

"So the question is, who baked them?" She studied the small piece that remained on her plate as if she were a jeweler examining a flawless diamond. "Let me guess. Either your mother, your mother's cook, your sister or an old nanny baked them."

"Nope."

"Then who?" she asked.

"I have a hot-shot programmer on my team named Christopher. He's a real rock star, but his hobby is baking."

"No way." She straightened. "I can't believe a computer geek baked these tasty morsels."

"It's true."

She snagged another brownie. "You'd better give the guy a raise or some restaurant is going to steal him away."

"I'd set him up with his own bakery before I let that happen."

She sighed.

"The brownies?" Bryce asked.

"No, you." She studied him with observant eyes. "I've never met anyone like you."

"Well, I've never met anyone like you, either." He appreciated her quick thinking and sense of humor. Not to mention her beauty. "I'm happy you're here."

"Me, too."

Bryce kissed her quickly, tasting chocolate and Dani.

The corners of her mouth curved. "Now that's the perfect end to this dinner."

"I suppose it's getting late."

She glanced out the window. "The rain is still coming down pretty hard out there."

"Do you want to wait it out by watching a movie?" he suggested. "There's a home theater and media room upstairs. That's the other room I had redone. Nothing better than playing video games on a large screen."

"Video games?" Interest flashed on her face. "Can we play instead of watching a movie?"

"You like games?"

"I love them."

The more time he spent with Dani, the more perfect she got. She was definitely a woman worth making time in his life for.

"I'd rather play video games than watch a movie any day," she added. "What platform do you have?"

"A Nintendo Wii and Xbox."

She shimmied her shoulders and stood. "I think I'm in heaven."

So was he. The lighting provided an alluring silhouette of her breasts. Bryce swallowed.

"A man after my own heart," she said.

Well, maybe not her heart, but he wouldn't mind a few of her other parts. Except he wasn't just after her body. He wanted Dani.

"So are you ready?" she asked.

Her question jerked his gaze away from her chest. She squared her shoulders and gave him a pointed look.

Okay, he deserved it. She'd caught him ogling her. But, hey, he was a guy. Men only had so much self-control. "Ready?"

For an apology, another brownie, a kiss…

Dani winked. "Ready to lose."

# CHAPTER NINE

Weapons blasted. Targets exploded. Pulse-pounding music blared. The button of the game controller toggled beneath Bryce's fingertip. "I am not going to lose."

Dani fired back. "Yes, you are."

He shot her a sideways glance.

Her breasts bounced. Her butt wiggled.

So hot. No wonder he kept losing with those sweet things to distract him. He needed to focus on the game instead.

"How did you get so good at video games?" he asked.

"The break room at my old job had all the different platforms for us to play."

Bryce launched one of his missiles, nearly wiping out Dani.

She sent a challenging look his way. "You are going down, Delaney."

"Think again, Bennett." A surge of adrenaline

sent Bryce jumping to his feet. Frustrated, yes. Defeated, no. He tapped faster, trying to fire shots in rapid succession. "You're the one who's going to be history."

"In your dreams." She fired a shot. Direct hit. His character exploded into red, orange and yellow flames. "Yes!"

"Nooooo!" he cried.

She raised her hands in the air. "I am officially the undefeated master—make that mistress—of the galaxies."

The title fit her, in more ways than one. Bryce tossed his controller onto one of the leather game chairs. "If you're expecting me to bow down before you—"

"I wasn't." Mischief gleamed in her eyes. "But now that you mention it…"

"You're a worthy opponent, but I don't get on my knees for anyone."

She winked. "We'll have to work on that."

Desire rocketed through him. "We could start now."

"I…" Dani glanced around the room, her eyes avoiding his. "It might be a little late for that."

Her coyness added to her sex appeal.

"Late is a relative term." He glanced at his watch and did a double take. "Though one o'clock in the morning is late by anyone's standards."

"It can't be that late."

"It is." He turned off the game console and

sound system, ready for whatever would come next. "We totally lost track of time. Do you know what this means?"

"Yes." She plopped into a chair and buried her face in her hands. "I've turned into a gamer geek."

"Then what does that make me?" he asked.

A grin replaced her look of despair. "With a choice setup like this, you're a gaming guru."

"I kind of like that, but not as much as I like having you here."

Dani blushed. Not exactly the reaction he was expecting from a gaming goddess but, then again, he never knew what to expect from her. At first that had bugged him, but now he could accept her unpredictable nature as just part of who she was.

She stood, lifted one of the blackout shades and peeked out. "It's still raining."

Bryce noticed the dark circles under her eyes and the wary lines around her mouth. He wanted her to stay, but only if she wanted to. "You're tired. I'll drive you home."

"Not in this rain. This late." She wrung her hands. "I'll call a cab."

"No cab," he said. "I drive you home or you spend the night."

She bit her lip.

"You don't have to sleep in my room. Unless you want." No way would Bryce rush things. Her. She should know that by now. He dragged his hand through his hair. "There's a guest room. You can borrow a pair of my pajamas. Heck, you can lock the door if that makes you more comfortable."

The corners of her mouth curved. "I don't mean to be difficult."

"And I'm not going to push you into anything you're not ready for."

Even if he might be ready for more.

The gratitude in her eyes made Dani's decision clear and, honestly, he was okay with that. Disappointed, but okay. He could see the two of them being together…a while.

"Not that I could make the mistress of the galaxies do anything she didn't want to do."

Dani laughed; the sound floated on the air and smacked him right in the gut.

"Smart man." Her tone sounded less tense. "So where's this guest room of yours?"

Bryce led her down the hall, making a quick stop at his room to grab her a pair of pajamas. "These are brand-new. Washed, never worn. I sleep in shorts and a T-shirt, but no matter how many times I tell my mother this she always buys me a pair of pajamas every Christmas."

"Thanks." Dani rubbed her fingers over the flannel fabric. "I usually wear a T-shirt to bed, but these are so soft they'll be a treat to sleep in."

The image of her wearing only a T-shirt sent his temperature up and made him wish she'd opted to sleep in his room instead.

"So which door…?" she asked.

Her words jostled him from the fantasy forming in his head.

"Right here." Bryce motioned to the closed door across from his. "In the bathroom drawer, you'll find toothbrushes and other stuff."

"Get a lot of overnight visitors?" she asked, her tone icy.

"Nope." He liked the idea she might be concerned about female visitors. And jealous. "I get a lot of freebies."

Her eyebrows raised.

He grinned. "From hotels and airlines. Help yourself to whatever you need."

"Thank you." She placed her hand on the doorknob. "Tonight has been so much fun."

Too bad the fun had to end. "Sleep well."

"You, too." She stared up through her lashes at him, her eyes full of affection. "Sweet dreams."

Bryce really wanted to kiss her goodnight, but she didn't want to rush things and he didn't trust himself not to. If she would only open the door and get away from him…

"Goodnight, Dani."

She rose on tiptoe and kissed his cheek. A chaste peck, really.

Not at all close to what Bryce wanted, but he'd take it.

Dani opened the door and stepped into the guest room. "Goodnight."

The shy, sweet smile on her face hit him like an arrow to his heart. He almost stumbled back.

She closed the door.

A good thing. Bryce leaned against the wall in the hallway. He blew out the breath he'd been holding.

Another second with her and he would have been on his knees.

Sunlight stole through cracks in the wooden blinds. Dani stretched her arms over her head. She couldn't believe how rested she felt. No doubt sleeping on a real mattress, complete with a pillow top, and not her hard futon, made the difference. She'd never known what sleeping on a cloud would feel like until last night. She could get used to this.

And Bryce.

Thinking about him brought a smile to her face. Dani owed him a home-cooked breakfast this morning for his hospitality. She was sure Bryce would have preferred a different sleeping arrangement last night. Yet he hadn't pushed her into something she wasn't comfortable with or ready for. She appreciated that. And him.

For all her talk of not wanting a boyfriend, she had to admit Bryce had quickly changed her mind. Funny, the thought of not being with him bothered her more than the realization she was dating someone.

Dani threw back the duvet-covered comforter. She wanted to see Bryce.

A quick stop in the bathroom, and she headed out of the room. Seeing Bryce's bedroom door closed, Dani walked softly down the stairs and into the kitchen. She didn't want to wake him.

"Good morning," a female voice greeted her.

Dani looked over at the kitchen table and saw a pretty young woman sitting there. She had dark hair and green eyes like Bryce. "Caitlin?"

"You know who I am, but I haven't a clue about you." A smile, complete with dimples on either side of her mouth, lit up the woman's face. "My brother is good at keeping secrets."

The word *secret* prickled the hair at the back of Dani's neck, but only warmth flowed from Caitlin.

"Not really a secret," Dani said. "I'm Dani Bennett."

An older woman with the same green eyes as Caitlin and Bryce but lighter hair strode into the kitchen with a cloud of expensive-smelling perfume in her wake. She carried a bag of frozen French fries. "His car is in the garage. He must have forgotten and slept…"

The woman's surprised gaze flicked over Dani with curiosity. "Who are you?"

"This is Dani Bennett," Caitlin said. "Dani, this is my mother, Maeve."

With expertly highlighted hair, porcelain skin and designer clothing, Bryce's mother radiated beauty and wealth. She studied Dani with sharp eyes, as if she were trying to decide if she'd found a masterpiece or a forgery.

Talk about intimidating. Awkward. Humiliating.

But Dani wasn't about to let nerves get the best of her. She owed it to Bryce and herself not to act overwhelmed. "It's nice to meet you, Mrs. Delaney."

"I haven't been a Delaney in decades." The woman's friendly smile caught Dani off guard and made her seem more like a mother than a matriarch. She placed the bag of fries in the freezer. "Call me Maeve, please."

"Thanks, Maeve," Dani said, trying out the name. "I'm a friend of Bryce's."

Maeve raised a finely arched brow. "More than a friend, I'd say, since you're wearing the pajamas I gave him for Christmas."

Embarrassed, Dani cringed. She could only imagine what Bryce's family thought she was doing here on a Saturday morning, wearing his pajamas.

"This isn't what you think. I mean, Bryce and I aren't... We didn't..."

Maeve laughed. "Then my son's not as smart a man as I thought he was. You're absolutely gorgeous."

An unwelcome heat crept into Dani's cheeks. She wished the ground would open up and swallow her. "Thank you."

"And modest, too," Caitlin said.

"Wherever did he find you, Dani?" Maeve asked.

Dani shifted her weight between her feet. "Blinddatebrides.com."

The two Delaney women smiled like a pair of Cheshire cats. They seemed happy over what they'd learned, not concerned.

Caitlin clapped her hands together. "Well, it's about time."

"I'll have to give Joelle a call," Maeve added.

Dani stood there, feeling as if they were speaking a foreign language.

"We've been telling Bryce to use his own site for dating since he founded it," Maeve explained. "But he says he's always working too much."

"Bryce does work hard," Dani said.

"We know," Caitlin said. "But he's always looking out for everyone else. It's nice to see that he's finally doing something for himself."

Maeve walked to the kitchen table and pulled out

a chair. "Come over here and sit down for a little chat, Dani. I want to hear all about you and my son."

"Uh…sure." Dani sat, making a silent cry for help. She might have handled Gymguy on her own and the mimes on the bus, but the two Delaney women, who looked as if they'd stepped from a window display at Neiman Marcus, absolutely terrified her.

Where was her backup when she really needed him?

Bryce hopped out of bed. Dani was in his house, in his guest bedroom. No reason to stay in his room alone. Not when he could see her and maybe snag a good-morning kiss.

He opened the door to his bedroom. Her door was ajar.

Bryce peeked inside. "Dani?"

No reply. Just an empty bed with the covers turned back. He made a beeline for the stairs.

Halfway down the steps, the sound of feminine laughter drifted up. Not just Dani, either.

His heart plummeted to his feet.

Today was Saturday. He was supposed to go out to breakfast with Caitlin and…

His mother.

Bryce sprinted down the stairs, taking them three at a time. Poor Dani. He loved his mother, but she wasn't known for her subtlety. He skidded into the kitchen.

The three women sat at the kitchen table with steaming coffee cups in front of them. Uh-oh, they'd been there a while.

"Good morning, ladies," he said.

Three heads turned toward him at the exact same time like a trio of synchronized swimmers. But one person wasn't wearing the same uniform as the other two.

His gaze focused on Dani, trying to assess any damage already afflicted upon her. At least she was smiling. And he didn't see any blood or bruises. Though her cheeks had more of a pink tinge than normal.

"Did you sleep well?" he asked.

"I did. Thanks." She looked into her coffee cup as if she could see the secrets to the universe inside. "I was coming down to get my clothes out of the dryer—"

"And she found us," Caitlin interrupted.

"I used my key," Maeve added. "I see you forgot about our breakfast date this morning."

The warmth in Dani's gaze made his senses reel. "I've been busy."

"I can see that." Maeve smiled. "But, this time, I understand why. We've enjoyed chatting with your…friend."

His mother emphasized the last word.

"Dani is my friend." Bryce didn't want Dani to feel uncomfortable, but that seemed impossible under the circumstances. "She and I are dating."

"You might have mentioned it," Maeve said. "Her."

"He hinted, Mother," Caitlin added. "Remember what I told you, but I'm sure he just wanted to keep Dani all to himself."

As the color on Dani's cheeks deepened to a bright red, Bryce's chest tightened. His sister was right. He did want to keep Dani for himself. He wanted to pull her away from his family and spend the morning with her. The afternoon and evening, too.

Caitlin leaned forward. "Dani, I don't know if Bryce has talked to you about—"

"Later," he interrupted.

"But—"

"I promise."

His sister nodded, her face glowing as if she were walking down the aisle today, not in nine months. "I have a great idea. What if the four of us go to breakfast and then Mother and I can take Dani shopping?"

"That would be a lovely way to spend the day," Maeve said. "We could stop in at the Fairmont afterward. The Laurel Court puts on a nice afternoon tea."

"Oh, afternoon tea would be perfect." Caitlin clasped her hands together. "We could always go to the Garden Court at the Palace Hotel. I love the harpist there."

Dani sat still, not saying a word. A smile remained frozen on her face, but her eyes reminded him of a deer caught in the headlights of two semitrucks approaching from opposite directions. No matter which way she went, she was going to get hit head-on.

Bryce wasn't about to let that happen.

He placed his hands on her shoulders and gave a reassuring squeeze.

"Of course, there's always the Ritz-Carlton," Maeve said. "What do you think, Dani?"

"Well, there's always Lovejoy's Tea Room in Noe Valley," she said before he could put a stop to the nonsense. "It has more of a cozy, eclectic feel, but they have a high tea on the menu and the most delicious scones."

Pride filled Bryce. Dani didn't need his help at all.

"I've been to Lovejoy's," Maeve said. "It's a charming teahouse."

Caitlin nodded. "One of my sorority sisters had her baby shower there. It was so much fun. I can call for reservations."

"Another time." Bryce rubbed Dani's shoulders. "We have plans for today."

With the wind on her face, Dani hung off the side of the cable car later that day. She was enjoying

Bryce's "plans." Who was she kidding? She couldn't have cared what they did as long as they were together.

The driver clanged the bell. And, like the old song her mother used to sing, zing went her heartstrings.

For Bryce.

She couldn't help herself. And that was…okay.

As she leaned farther away from the car, he tightened his hand around her waist.

Always the protector.

Dani didn't mind today. She glanced back at him. "I can't believe you were born in San Francisco and have never ridden a cable car. That's downright criminal."

He shrugged. "What can I say? I've never played tourist in my own town."

"You don't know what you're missing."

"I'm getting an idea."

So was she. Dani grinned, looking up at the overcast sky. More rain might be predicted, but she didn't care. The day was perfect, no matter what the forecast. The only thing missing—a rainbow.

The cable car stopped. Passengers disembarked. Bryce jumped off and extended his hand. Her fingers clasped his as he helped her down.

Pleasurable sensations of wanting tingled through her.

"Thank you for showing me San Francisco." He

raised her hand to his mouth and kissed it. The beat of her heart quadrupled. "Fisherman's wharf, North Beach, Chinatown—"

"And now Union Square," she finished for him. "Though this is more your part of town so it's your turn to show me around."

Bryce took over as tour guide, leading her across Union Square. He stopped in front of a tall winged statue. "This is the goddess Victory. You and she have a lot in common."

Dani raised a brow. "Trying to soften me up with compliments?"

"It's either that or I'll have to buy you some chocolate."

"You've got me figured out pretty well."

He smiled. "I'm working on it."

And she knew he was. That pleased her.

The sounds of cars, trucks and buses on the four streets surrounding the square were loud, but Dani heard music. The haunting sounds of a lone violin filled the air. She looked around. A violinist stood on the corner. She smiled. That was one thing she loved about the city—the unexpected.

"There's something I've been wondering," Bryce said.

She focused her attention on him. "What?"

"How does an evening of mayhem with my crazy

family and over two hundred of my mother's most intimate acquaintances sound?"

"Is this a trick question?" she asked.

"No. My mother is throwing Caitlin and Mark an engagement party next Saturday. Would you like to go?"

A family event? Dani quivered with excitement. "Yes, I'd like that very much. Thanks."

"Thank you." Relief filled his eyes. "If you'd said no, I don't think Caitlin would have forgiven me."

"Then it's a good thing I said yes."

With a nod, he led her to a crosswalk in the city's downtown shopping district. They stood on the corner waiting for the lights to change.

"You've got to promise me you won't hold my family against me, though. The Delaneys are an odd cast of characters. I come from a line of men who foresaw what land in San Francisco and the surrounding Bay Area would be worth someday. They bought as much as they could, whenever they could and held on to it. Thanks to their real estate acumen, my relatives now live off trust funds."

"Not you."

"I've never touched mine and my family can't understand why," he admitted. "I did accept my house. A graduation present from the family trust. But, like you, I want to make it on my own."

Her respect for Bryce shot off the scale. "You really do understand what I want to do."

"I told you we weren't so different."

She was beginning to think he was right. Dani smiled. "You did."

"And, as I've said before, I admire your determination."

His compliment sent a welcome shot of confidence flowing through her.

The light turned green. She stepped off the curb into the street. She jogged around a woman pushing a baby stroller and drinking from a Starbucks cup as they crossed the intersection.

Dani followed him through a white iron gate to a pedestrian-only narrow street dotted with umbrella-shaded tables.

"Maiden Lane used to be the red light district during the Barbary Coast era so I'm not sure where the 'Maiden' part came from," Bryce said, as tourists in baseball caps and sunglasses snapped pictures. He clasped his hand with hers. "But the street has become more upscale since then."

As she strolled with Bryce, Dani noticed the signs of the expensive boutiques and salons. Women dressed as if they were going to a fancy party and loaded down with shopping bags darted in and out of the shops. Even when Dani had earned more money at her last job, she hadn't shopped here. "It's nice."

"This is nice." Bryce rubbed her hand with his thumb. "I never thought I'd find someone I wanted to date using my own Web site."

"Me, either," she admitted. "I was pretty anti-dating."

"And now?"

A man in a fluorescent orange warm-up suit walked a tiny black dog.

"Not so much."

He smiled. "I'm happy we met, Dani Bennett."

"Me, too."

She noticed a pretty green dress displayed on a mannequin in the window of a boutique. She stopped to take a closer look. Now, that would be something to wear to the engagement party if she wanted to make a good impression.

"That's a pretty dress."

Dani nodded.

He pulled her over to the window. "Do you want to try it on?"

She shook her head. "New clothing isn't in my budget right now."

"You can still try the dress on," he said.

She shot him a look.

He made a face. "Don't tell me you've never window-shopped. Caitlin dragged me along on one of her arduous excursions and she said trying on clothes is half the fun, whether you buy them or not."

"I don't know." She stepped back. "There's no chance of me buying anything in there."

Bryce pulled her to the door. "Come on."

"I—"

"Trust me. It'll be fun."

Dani found herself inside an elegant boutique with pale green walls and gilded fixtures. Cheerful music from a string quartet played. The air smelled of flowers and money. All the women were dressed to the nines. She couldn't tell who was a customer or who worked there and felt out of place wearing her work clothes from yesterday. A tall, thin woman with long red hair walked toward them.

"Pick a few things to try on," he encouraged.

Dani selected two dresses, neither of which had price tags attached.

Bryce handed her a third. "I want to see how the color looks on you."

She shrugged. "Why not?"

"That's the spirit." He sat in a big overstuffed chair.

Gabrielle, the redhead, who looked more like a supermodel than a clothing salesperson, handed him a drink. "Fashion show time."

In the dressing room, Dani found matching shoes, compliments of Gabrielle, to try on with each of the dresses and changed into the green dress from the window.

"Come out here so I can see," Bryce called.

Dani studied herself in a full-length mirror. "It's a little short."

"I'd like to be the judge of that myself."

"Oh, boy." She wedged her feet into the coordinating shoes, heels higher than she normally wore, with more crystals than she could count, and teetered out of the dressing room. "Too short?"

"I was going to say just right." He grinned like a kid turned loose in a Lego store. "No more hiding those long legs of yours, okay?"

"I usually wear pants."

Bryce waved her off. "Try on the next dress."

Dani squeezed into a red cocktail dress. The halter neck style really accentuated her breasts, making her look like a hooker who might have worked this street during the city's bygone era. She gulped.

"Do you have it on?" Bryce asked.

"On is relative," she admitted. "There isn't much fabric."

"Out—now," he said, sounding impatient.

She jammed her feet into a pair of stilettos, afraid to look in the mirror, and carefully walked out of the dressing room so she wouldn't topple over.

Bryce's eyes widened. "Wow."

"Don't you think it's a bit…skimpy?" she asked.

"You look hot, but I'm sure there'd be a fight or two if you wore that out in public. But the dress would be great for an intimate dinner for two at home."

"I'd rather wear your sweats," she admitted.

"Comfort over style."

Dani smiled. "You know it."

"Are you having fun yet?" Bryce asked.

She nodded.

Satisfaction gleamed in his eyes. "Let's see the next one."

In the dressing room, she wiggled into the blue cocktail dress Bryce had selected. She stared at herself in the mirror, not recognizing her reflection.

She looked and felt like a princess. A warmth settled in the center of her chest. Was this how Marissa had felt when she'd finally found her wedding dress?

Dani slipped on the pair of silver slingback heels that actually fit and were reasonably comfortable for heels.

Feeling like the heroine from an animated movie, she pirouetted out of the dressing room.

"Stunning." Bryce leaned forward, cradling his drink in his hands. "That's my favorite."

"Mine, too." She touched the soft fabric with her fingertip. "But I'd better put on my own clothes in case someone wants to buy it."

In the changing room, Dani stepped out of the shoes. The other two dresses and shoes had been removed from the changing room.

Gabrielle handed her a glass of sparkling mineral water with a slice of lime. "For you."

The places where Dani shopped limited taking clothing into a dressing room to six items or fewer. The only thing the attendants handed customers were plastic numbers. She placed the drink on the small table in her dressing room. "Thanks."

"May I please have your dress once you have it off so I can put it on the hanger?"

"Sure." Dani closed the curtain and took off the dress. She reluctantly handed it through the slit in the drapes to a waiting Gabrielle.

"Thank you, Dani."

"You're welcome."

This was like no window-shopping expedition she'd ever been on before. Even the dressing room was luxurious, with silk curtains, overstuffed benches and gilded mirrors.

Dani put on her own clothing and walked out to find an empty chair. She looked around the shop. Bryce stood by the door with a glossy bag in his hand.

Her heart fell. "You didn't."

"The blue dress was made for you."

Dani started to speak, but noticed people staring at them. She exited the store. Bryce followed, carrying the bag.

"We were window-shopping, not buying," she said.

"That's before I saw you in the dress."

She stopped in front of the store next door. "I appreciate your thoughtfulness, but I don't feel comfortable with you buying me clothing."

"It's a gift," he said as if he'd bought her a latte at the corner coffee shop and not a designer cocktail dress and, guessing by the box in the bag, the shoes, too. "I'm sure you have something nice you could wear to the engagement party, but I wanted to do something special for you. Is that wrong?"

He looked so pleased with himself. She didn't want to hurt his feelings. "It's very sweet of you, but it's important to me that I do things myself. Buy things myself."

"Do you buy gifts for yourself?"

"No."

"You don't like gifts."

Dani noticed it wasn't a question. "I'm not really used to getting gifts."

"It's time for that to change." Bryce hugged her. His soap and water scent made her heady. "Let's start today."

She loved being in his embrace, with his strong arms wrapped around her. He made her feel safe and secure, as if he'd never let anything happen to her. She'd never felt this way with anyone before. And she liked the feeling. A little too much.

Dani stepped back. "I'm—"

"Not trying to be difficult," he finished for her. "Neither am I."

Stalemate.

She didn't know what to say or do. Her gaze strayed to the shopping bag. She looked away.

"You know, I took your advice and checked out some of those dating articles on the Web site you mentioned," Bryce said. "Compromise is the key to a successful relationship."

"Are we in a relationship?" she asked.

"You've worn my clothes, kissed me until I couldn't see straight, spent the night at my house and charmed my family." He smiled. "If we aren't in a relationship, we're pretty darn close."

The air whooshed from her lungs. This was more than she'd hoped for. She stared up at him. The affection in his eyes matched how she felt about him.

"What do you say now?" Bryce asked.

This was the last thing she'd thought she wanted, but a wellspring of joy flowed through her, settling at the center of her chest. Dani looked back at the shopping bag. "I guess I'd better learn to compromise."

# CHAPTER TEN

To: "Englishcrumpet"
<englishcrumpet@blinddatebrides.com>
"Kangagirl" <kangagirl@blinddatebrides.com>
From: "Dani"
<sanfrandani@blinddatebrides.com>
Subject: You won't believe this!

I got your messages. Sorry I've missed our chats. I've been with Bryce. We're back together and spending all our free time together this week!!! Dinners, movies. I even taught him how to make bonbons. It's been incredible. He's such an amazing person. I know it's a little soon, but I think he might be the one. My one. Can you believe it? I'm attending his sister's engagement party tonight. Cross your fingers I make a good impression on his family. I'm nervous about that. I'll fill you in on all the details later. Hope all is well with you. Miss you! xoxox
-d

"I'M ALMOST ready."

Saturday night, Bryce heard Dani's panicky voice through the closed door to her walk-in closet. He didn't mind waiting. Anything to make things easier on her. "No rush."

To tell the truth, he was nervous, too, and dreading the evening ahead. All his extended family would be there. He felt like an outsider when the whole clan was together so he was glad to be bringing Dani with him. She understood him better than his own family ever had.

"Is the press really going to be there?" she asked from behind the closet door.

"Yes. Delaney events usually bring out the society columnists, but since I founded Blinddate-brides.com because of my sister and now she's met her future husband at the site, the engagement has become a human interest story."

"It's pretty unbelievable."

No kidding. And he didn't only mean Caitlin's engagement.

Bryce hadn't brought home a woman in almost five years. That had been his last "serious" relationship until its daytime talk show worthy breakup. He'd been dating casually—okay, sporadically—since then, but hadn't wanted another relationship. Not until he'd met Dani. And now he kept thinking he might have found more than just a girlfriend on Blinddatebrides.com himself.

The door to the closet opened. Footsteps tapped on the hardwood floor. Dani's heels.

Bryce turned.

Hot! Attraction hit fast and hard, sending his already warm blood into the red zone. "I didn't think you could look more beautiful than you did at the store. I was wrong."

Dani radiated beauty and warmth. He'd picked out the dress because the color matched her eyes. But the style accentuated pretty much every other part of her body. "You are totally captivating and very sexy."

And his.

Dani spun around on the balls of the silver sling-back shoes. The fabric of her dress wrapped around her hips and thighs. The asymmetric hem made her legs look even longer. She gave a slight curtsy. "Thank you."

Her shy smile contrasted against her curvaceous body was a total turn-on. "If my father hits on you, I'm going to slug him."

"Don't worry, I'm too old for him."

Bryce's gaze lingered as he went from the top of her shiny blond hair to the V between her breasts to the curve of her hips to her delicate ankles and her hot-pink painted toenails. His heart rate kicked up a notch. No doubt other men's would, too. A protective instinct kicked in. "A couple of extra years won't matter in your case. But he's not the only one I'm worried about."

"Well…" Mischief gleamed in her eyes. "On the farm, parties never got going until a fight happened."

He laughed. "The Delaney crowd is much too civilized for throwing actual punches. They resort to verbal barbs to one's face and gossip behind one's back instead."

"Sounds like high school."

"Pretty close." The look of vulnerability flashing across her face brought him to her side in an instant. Bryce wrapped his arms around her. "But you won't have to worry about a thing. I'll be right there with you to make sure you feel safe and comfortable."

Dani gazed up at him. "I figured you weren't the kind of guy to desert me while he went off to socialize."

"Never. I have everything I need right here." He brushed his lips across the top of her hair. The scent of grapefruit filled his nostrils. "Is it totally sexist of me to say I'm going to like having the sexiest, most beautiful woman at the party on my arm?"

"Yes." A seductive smile spread across her shimmering glossed lips. "But since I'll be on the arm of the hottest man at the soirée, I'll let it slide.

"Soirée?"

She shrugged. "When in Rome…"

"You're going to fit in just fine, Miss Bennett."

Dani fluttered her eyelashes. "Why, thank you, Mr. Delaney."

He extended his arm, no longer dreading the evening ahead. "Shall we?"

Maeve Delaney-Stuart-Whitney-Roya-Mayer's house reminded Dani of Pemberley, with its marble floors, crystal chandeliers and uniformed servants milling about with trays of champagne and hors d'oeuvres. Dani glanced around the mansion, trying to imagine Bryce, an active and inquisitive little boy, growing up among the valuable artwork and antiques.

Tried and failed.

Standing at the doorway to a balcony, she watched Bryce weave his way through the crowded room with two drinks in his hands. He looked suave and debonair in his tailored suit, white shirt and tie. He stood out from the others. It wasn't his height or his looks, but his presence. He exuded power and, though he'd disagree with her, wealth. People followed him, trying to get his attention or catch his eye. Men who wanted his advice. Women who wanted him.

Dani didn't blame them. She wanted him, too.

Bryce said a word to one, nodded to another and continued toward her, his steps never faltering and his gaze never leaving hers.

Outside on the patio, he handed her a Cosmopolitan. "Did the animals leave you alone while I was gone?"

"I had a couple of close calls, but I survived unscathed."

A man with his tie askew yelled Bryce's name from the doorway. Bryce acknowledged him with a wave, then lowered his hand. His fingertips stroked her arm, sending tingles shooting up and down from the point of contact. "What happened?"

"Nothing you need to worry about. It was more funny than awkward."

"I just want to make sure you're comfortable."

"I'm better than comfortable." She raised her glass. "I'm Cinderella at the ball with Prince Charming at my side."

"At least you won't have to worry about the clock striking midnight," he teased. "Your dress and ride home have no expiration time."

"Good to know." She stared up into his concerned eyes. "What?"

"Please tell me what happened while I was gone."

"It was nothing."

Bryce raised a brow.

"If you really want to know, your cousin Simone

asked me who did my breast augmentation because she thought they looked so natural."

"She's been redoing herself part by part," he explained. "Breasts are next."

"No wonder she seemed so disappointed to find out mine are real, but I appreciated the compliment."

"You should." He eyed her chest momentarily. "Anything else?"

"I bumped into your great-uncle Edward. Or he bumped into me." Dani grinned. "I think he wanted to cop a feel."

"He's known for that."

She took a sip of the pink-colored drink. The martini was strong. Better limit herself to two tonight. Especially since they'd already drank champagne during a toast to Caitlin and Mark. "See, it was nothing."

"I'm not leaving you again," Bryce said. "I told you I wouldn't desert you."

"I told you I wanted a drink, but didn't feel like pushing my way through the crowd to the bar. It's okay," she said. "I'm doing fine. I was intimidated when we arrived, but everyone has been so welcoming, especially your mother. Things have been much better than I imagined. And Caitlin and Mark are such a cute couple and so nice."

"That's because they, and the rest of my family, like you."

Music played. She couldn't tell if it was a live band or a DJ. "Good, because I like them."

"Even my great-uncle Edward?" Bryce asked.

She nodded. "He's funny. He told me if he were fifty years younger he'd give you a run for your money over me. Then he said if I wanted to fly to Las Vegas and marry him tonight he wouldn't make me sign a prenup."

"What did you tell him?" Bryce asked.

"I told him I couldn't desert my date tonight, but if things didn't work out with you, we could talk later."

Bryce laughed. "No wonder he stopped me on my way back from the bar and asked my intentions toward you."

"Oh, no." She cringed. "I thought he knew I was kidding."

"I'm sure he did, but hope springs eternal, especially when enchanting young women are involved," Bryce said. "His words, not mine."

Dani smiled.

"So is this the woman who Edward called dibs on?" A handsome man with black hair and green eyes approached. Dressed in a tuxedo, he looked like an older, bronzed version of Bryce. "Hello, son."

Bryce's eyes narrowed. He placed his hand on Dani's lower back. "Father, this is Dani Bennett. Dani, my father, Peter."

Peter kissed the top of her hand, holding on to it

too long to be considered proper or polite. "Edward wasn't kidding. You are stunning."

The man looked at her as if she were the special of the day he could order off the menu, not his son's date. "Thank you."

A photographer asked them to pose. Dani stood between the two Delaney men, both of whom had an arm around her. The flash of the camera blinded her.

She blinked.

When the spots went away, she noticed Peter checking her out. Bryce might resemble Peter in looks, but that was where the similarities ended. His father exuded charm, but his tone and mannerisms came off as too smooth. Too practiced. Too superficial.

No wonder Peter Delaney went for younger woman. Any older female would see right through his gentlemanly façade to the player underneath. He seemed like the type of guy who would trade in wives along with his cars when their leases expired.

Dani appreciated Bryce's protective, almost possessive hand on her, and inched closer.

"Don't get all territorial on me, son," Peter teased. "I promise not to steal this one away from you."

This one? Dani thought.

"Not that you don't have excellent taste. But your last girlfriend cost me a bundle." Peter laughed. "Of course, she would have cost more if I'd married her."

Ick.

"It's not marriage that cost you, Father. It's the divorces," Bryce said dryly.

"What can I say? I'm a sucker for a beautiful woman. And so, apparently, are you." Peter smiled again at Dani.

His words rankled. "Bryce is no sucker, Mr. Delaney. Not that I would ever try to sucker him in the first place."

Peter's eyes widened. "A woman with a sharp tongue who speaks her mind, eh?"

"Dani's more than beautiful," Bryce said. "She's also smart."

"Then you'll need to watch yourself even more, son." Peter appraised her from head to toe. "Those smart ones are dangerous."

No doubt the history between these two involved more than your typical father/son issues. She wondered if Bryce had gotten over what had happened or if that was why an attractive man like him was still single.

Sipping her drink, Dani stared at the two men.

An undercurrent charged the air.

"I'm not worried," Bryce said finally.

"Maybe you should be." Peter's gaze bounced between her and Bryce. "Well, I'm off to find my fiancée. She's probably gotten herself lost trying to find the restroom."

"Same thing happened when she was here for one of Caitlin's sleepovers in high school." Bryce raised his glass. "Good luck."

"You, too." Peter turned his attention on Dani again. Her breasts, actually. "It was a pleasure meeting you. Catch you two later."

He disappeared into the crowd.

"Sorry about that," Bryce said.

"No worries." She had questions, lots of them, but tonight was neither the time nor place to ask about something that had happened long before she'd entered the picture. "Let's just enjoy the party."

He kissed her cheek. "Come on."

"Are we going to meet more people?"

"Nope." Bryce held her hand and led her inside and through the throng of guests toward the door. "Cinderella should dance at the ball."

She stopped. "You don't like to dance."

He grinned. "But you do."

Later that night, Bryce stood with Dani at the door of her apartment. This was only the beginning for them. "Tonight was…"

"Magical," she finished for him, then rose on tiptoe to kiss him on the lips.

Magical was right. Especially her kiss.

"Thank you so much for inviting me to the engagement party and dancing with me," she said, her cheeks flushed and her eyes sparkling. "I had the best time."

"Uncle Edward and my father aside."

"Uncle Edward was cute."

"And harmless. My father, however, is the ultimate player," Bryce explained. "He doesn't respect women or treat them well, but he has enough money he's willing to spend that some don't mind."

"Like your girlfriend?"

"Ex-girlfriend," Bryce clarified. "She had her eyes on my father from the beginning and used me to get to him."

"I'm sorry." Dani reached up and caressed his face. "I hope you know I would never…"

"I trust you, Dani."

He kissed her gently, soaking up the feel and taste of her. And then something changed. Something in him ignited, catching fire. He couldn't get enough of her kiss—of her. With his hands in her hair, he backed her up against the door. She pressed against him. His lips moved over hers. Dani tugged at his shirt, impatient. She was with him all the way.

Bryce pulled back to look her in the eyes; her pupils expanded.

Her face flushed, she moistened her swollen lips. "I think we know where this is going."

"I hope so."

That shy smile of hers appeared. "I really like

you, Bryce. I want to invite you in, but I don't want to make any mistakes or do something we might regret later if we go too fast."

Not what he wanted to hear, but so what? She was worth waiting for.

He took a deep breath. And another.

"You are a smart one." Bryce looked into her eyes. His affection for Dani grew with each passing second. "We've got plenty of time ahead of us."

"Us," she repeated, her eyes twinkling.

Bryce nodded. He liked the sound of *us*. More than he'd thought he would.

"And, for the record," he said, running his finger along her jawline, "I like you, too."

On Monday, the clock still hadn't struck midnight. Sure, Dani was back in her routine and at work, but she felt as if she were still floating from Saturday night. The entire weekend, really. She'd joined Bryce and his family for brunch on Sunday. All of the Delaneys made her feel so welcome. And Bryce made her feel so…loved.

Forget about falling for him.

She'd fallen, body and soul.

Dani might as well wrap her heart in pretty paper, tie the package with a neat bow and stick a tag with Bryce's name on it.

Could love happen so quickly?

Marissa and Grace thought so. Dani wanted to believe, too. She didn't know what else this all-consuming wonderfulness could be.

An emergency meeting at Blinddatebrides.com meant she couldn't see Bryce tonight, but he'd called, texted and e-mailed her. That had kept a wide smile on her face the rest of the day at work.

At her apartment, Dani found a breathtaking bouquet of stargazer lilies waiting for her with a note:

Thinking of you. Missing you. Can't wait to see you. B.

Happiness consumed her. Definitely love. She held on to the vase and swirled. She couldn't wait to hop onto chat and tell her friends. A happy ending might be in her future after all. She sure hoped so.

Tuesday morning, Dani sat in her cubicle, thinking of ways to build the Hookamate.com community. Even though she had two job interviews, courtesy of Bryce's contacts, lined up for later in the week, she wouldn't allow herself to do a lousy job at Hookamate.com, even if she hated working here. She'd made up for not going on any more dates by writing some killer content for the site that had earned her high fives from the engineers.

But each ping from her e-mail in-box captured her attention. She wanted to hear from Bryce, even though she was meeting him for lunch in less than an hour.

"I knew you were good, Danica," James said from the opening of her cubicle. "I just didn't know how good."

She kept working at her computer. "Is revenue up again this month?"

"Yes, and traffic, too, but that's not what I'm talking about." Paper crinkled. "Way to go, getting on the inside. I've got to hand it to you, Danica. I didn't know you had it in you."

The approval in his voice made her nervous. Made her turn. He held a copy of the *Life* section of the newspaper in his hand. "What are you talking about?"

He showed her the society page, specifically a picture of her with Bryce and his father. The description identified her as the date of Bryce Delaney, CEO of Blinddatebrides.com.

Her stomach roiled. She hadn't wanted James to find out about her and Bryce this way. Not until she had a new job and was ready to quit.

"Congrats on hooking a really big fish," her boss said. "What kind of inside info have you found out?"

Inside info?

And then she realized… James thought she was using Bryce for information, not dating him for real.

"Nothing. I—"

"Take your time." Excitement filled James's voice. "Get him to trust you."

Dani raised her chin. "Bryce already trusts me."

"So soon? You must be good."

She frowned at James's suggestive tone. "I'm not dating Bryce to get information. I really like him. Our jobs have no impact on us."

At least no longer. Thank goodness.

"Perhaps not on him, but you can use this to *our* advantage."

The emphasis on the word *our* made her straighten. "I'm sorry, James, but I can't do that to Bryce or myself. I have more ethics than that."

"Ethics, huh." James's features hardened. His eyes narrowed. He stood, towering above her, boldly intimidating. "Don't forget you signed a non-disclosure agreement and a non-compete clause when you accepted this position."

"So?" Dani asked.

"So if you're not getting info out of Bryce, I will have to assume you're spying on Hookamate for him. And that's a job-terminating offense."

Bryce hated seeing Dani so torn up. He sat next to her on a park bench and put his arm around her. "But James didn't actually fire you."

"No." Dani's voice trembled. She clasped her hands together. No doubt if she hadn't, she'd be wringing them. "Not yet anyway, but his intent was clear. I use my being your new girlfriend to get info or I lose my job."

"That's blackmail." Anger burned. She didn't deserve to be treated this way. "James is using you to get to me. He's had it in for me ever since I quit and founded Blinddatebrides.com. That's the only reason he decided to start his own online dating Web site."

"Did you know he won't even say the name of your Web site? He calls it bdb.com."

"The guy is an idiot." Bryce pulled Dani against him. "Just quit. I'll cover your expenses until you find a new job."

She straightened, drawing away from him. "I appreciate the offer, but I can deal with James on my own."

Her independence was admirable, but unnecessary. "This isn't only about you now. I feel responsible for what's happened. And I know James better than you—"

"Please don't," Dani urged. "You're Caitlin's big brother, not mine."

"My feelings for you aren't at all brotherly."

Dani's hair caught on the wind. Simply beautiful.

Who was Bryce kidding? There was nothing simple about her. She was complex, challenging and even difficult at times. He wouldn't have her any other way.

"I care about you, Dani."

"I care about you, too, but it's my job at stake. You remember how I told you my father left us?"

Bryce nodded.

"Well, my mother had relied on him for everything. When he took off, she was left with nothing except the four of us girls. She'd dropped out of college to get married, never worked a day in her life and didn't even know their checking account number. She learned her lesson and wanted to make sure me and my sisters didn't repeat her mistakes. She taught us to take charge of our own lives and ourselves. That's what I've been trying to do. That's what I need to do with James. I can handle this." Her eyes implored him. "I need to handle this."

He squeezed her hand reassuringly. "You can handle anything."

"Thanks for understanding. That means…a lot to me."

"I do understand, but just know I'm here if you need backup."

"Okay."

But, back in his office, he wasn't so sure. James's behavior had everything to do with Bryce and Blinddatebrides.com, not Dani. He hated seeing her caught in the middle and wanted to keep her from getting hurt.

Bryce knew she was attending an afternoon training class off-site when he arrived at Hookamate.com.

James didn't look surprised to see him. "You're here about Danica."

Bryce seethed with anger, but losing control wouldn't solve anything. The last time he'd lost his temper and argued with Dani, he'd almost lost her. He wasn't about to do that again.

He set his jaw, determined to put an end to James's dirty dealings, once and for all. "Stop taking out your problems with me on Dani. Keep her out of this and stay away from my company or I'll bring legal action against you."

"You have no proof." James glowered. "No prosecutor would touch the case."

"They will if Dani testifies."

"Is that all the wunderkind Bryce Delaney can come up with? A frivolous lawsuit to spend his trust fund on." James cackled. "You think a jury would believe a disgruntled former employee who's sleeping with my top competitor?"

Bryce's blood ran cold. "Former employee?"

"Why, yes." James smirked. "If there was any wrongdoing, Danica's involved. What else can I do, but fire her?"

Fired.

Dani's shoulders sagged and her bottom lip quivered.

Bryce hadn't listened to her. He hadn't trusted her

to handle James on her own. Even after she'd explained why she needed to.

Carrying the box containing items from her desk and cubicle, Dani trudged up the stairs of her apartment building.

*I thought more of you, Danica. I never expected you would send your lover in to fight your battle.*

James's words splintered her heart.

She'd lost everything in one fell swoop.

Because her boss was a jackass.

Because her boyfriend was a control freak.

Because she was a starry-eyed idiot.

How could she let this happen?

Dani had spent her entire life trying to make something of herself. To be someone. To do everything on her own so she'd never be in the same position as her mother had years ago.

Yet she'd trusted Bryce, believed in him and that had cost Dani her job. And…

Her heart.

Tears pricked her eyes. She blinked them away.

Turning the corner, Dani spotted Bryce.

Concern clouded his eyes. "Dani—"

Just for a moment, she longed to sink against him, to have him hold her and make everything better, but that would make James's accusations true. She wasn't going to rely on Bryce. She couldn't.

Dani swallowed around the gigabyte-sized lump clogging her throat. "Go away."

"We have to talk."

Raw pain stabbed her heart. Dani fought against the sting of tears. She was suddenly six years old, standing on the driveway as her dad loaded his suitcases in the trunk. *I love you, Danica. I love all of you. I'll come back. Promise.*

But he hadn't and didn't.

Her dad had said one thing and done another.

Just like Bryce.

Her chest tightened as if being squeezed by an extra-large vice grip. "Why should I believe anything you have to say to me now?"

Bryce's gaze sought hers. "You're upset."

"Damn right I am."

He pressed his lips together in a thin line. "I don't want to argue about this. Fighting won't solve anything."

His coolness and rationality irritated her. Her heart pounded. Her heart ached. Every nerve ending shrieked. And he stood there acting like Mr. Cool. "Neither do I."

"Good. Let's—"

"You don't get it." *Or me.* The unspoken words scorched her throat. "I don't want to talk to you."

"Don't do this, Dani."

Dani fumbled with her keys, opened the door and

hurried inside. She dropped the box. It thudded against the floor. Sort of like her heart had done when James told her Bryce had stopped by and she was fired. "You cost me my job."

"James cost you your job." Bryce followed her inside the apartment and closed the door behind him. "That guy is a sleaze."

"That guy is—was—my boss."

"You deserve a better one."

"Maybe. Or maybe I deserve a better boyfriend."

His expression froze for a moment. "I have a lead on a job opening. A great opportunity for you. I talked to a friend this afternoon—"

"You mean you went behind my back. Again."

He frowned. "If you mean James, I did you a favor."

"A favor?" She squared her shoulders. "You did the exact opposite of what I asked you to do."

"Yeah." Bryce exhaled. "I'm sorry. I was trying to protect—"

"Your company?"

"My company, my employees. And you."

She took a deep breath, trying to keep herself together, when all she wanted to do was shout and cry. "I don't need you to protect me."

"Yeah, you do."

"I don't want you to protect me," she clarified.

"What you want and what you need are two different things."

She rubbed her tight neck. "I told you I needed to take care of this myself."

"I told you, I was trying to protect you."

His calm manner sent her temper soaring. "You don't want to protect. You want to control. Me, Caitlin, every single one of your clients on Blinddatebrides.com with that stupid matching program of yours."

His mouth twisted. "That program said we were highly compatible."

"There must be a bug in the code." Dani stared down her nose at him. "I need someone who respects my independence."

His eyes darkened, the green turning into that of a stormy sea. "You care more about your damn independence than our relationship."

"What relationship?" she countered, crossing her apartment to put much-needed distance between them. "You want me to trust your judgment about James and my job, but there's no commitment between us. You've said we're dating, but you've never called me your girlfriend or asked us to be exclusive or said…"

"Those are just words." He took a step toward her, then stopped. "What I do is more important than what I say. I did what I thought was best for you today."

Tears choked Dani. "You have no idea what's best for me."

A muscle throbbed at his temples. "I can fix this."

"You've done enough." She stood in one corner with an ocean of room separating her from Bryce. "I've fallen in love with you, but being with you has never been about what your wealth and influence could do for me. By going to James the way you did, you acted as if it was. As if I were no different than any of the women your father marries and divorces."

Bryce's nostrils flared. "I'm nothing like my father."

"No, you're like mine. Promising one thing and doing another."

He made a fist with his hands, then stretched out his fingers. "You won't let me do anything for you."

"That's because you want to do everything for me."

Dani waited for him to deny it. He didn't.

"I…" Her voice cracked. "I want you to go."

Bryce's jaw clenched. "I know I overstepped, Dani, but is this what you really want?"

No. She wanted him to say he loved her, even though she was angry with him. She wanted him to say he would never leave her, even though she'd told him to go away.

She wanted…the impossible.

Her pounding heart felt as if it might explode.

Dani might want those things from Bryce; she might want him. But she didn't need him; she didn't need anyone.

She raised her chin. "Yes, I want you to go."

# CHAPTER ELEVEN

DANI took a deep breath. Her fingers trembled on her laptop keyboard. She typed…

To: "Grace", "Marissa"
From: "Dani"
Subject: Hey!
Thanks for the e-mails and IMs. I knew you guys would understand why I had to cancel my Blinddatebrides account and make a clean break. My landlord found someone who wanted an apartment ASAP so I packed up and rented a truck. I'm now at my mom's trying to regroup. Sorry I can't chat. Dial-up sucks. Hope you both are well. Miss you! TTYS.
Love,
Dani

She hit "send" and logged off so her mom could receive phone calls. No DSL or cable to connect to the Internet at her mom's trailer.

It was strange being back on the farm.

Dani had been here two days. It felt like two years the way time was passing so slowly, and she was hurting so badly.

She'd gone from standing on the edge of forever, of having the elusive pot of gold at the end of the rainbow within her grasp, to falling into an endless spiral of regrets, heartache and tears.

Lots and lots of tears.

She missed Bryce more than she'd thought possible. And she felt as if she had only herself to blame.

Something clanged outside.

Dani rose from the kitchen table and walked to the window. Outside, the wind chime they'd made out of silverware for their mom on Mother's Day hung on a rusted nail. A fork with missing tines blew into a bended spoon. She laughed.

"Now that's a sound I like to hear." Dolly Bennett spoke with a Southern accent even though she'd only spent the first twenty years of her life in Mississippi. "There hasn't been enough laughter around here since you all moved away."

"I can't believe you kept that old wind chime, Mom."

"That's a masterpiece, darlin'. No way could I get rid of it." Her mom handed Dani a plate with freshly baked chocolate-chip cookies. "I know these are your favorites. Maybe they'll help you find that beautiful smile of yours."

Dani set the plate on the table behind her and took a bite of one. The still warm chocolate chips melted in her mouth. "Thanks, Mom. For the cookies. For letting me come here and stay."

"No thanks are necessary. You always have a place here." Her mother smoothed Dani's hair. "This is your home, no matter where you end up making your mark on the world."

"Home."

Dolly pulled her into a hug. "And it feels a lot more homey when you girls are here with me. That's for sure."

Emotion welled within Dani. For so long, she'd been searching and dreaming about finding a place to call home when, in fact, she'd had one all along.

Home wasn't something you bought, but the place where you were surrounded by love. Whether a house or a beat-up station wagon or an old two bedroom, one bath single-wide trailer.

She was home.

An unfamiliar contentment filled her.

And this was the perfect place to pull herself together and figure out what she wanted to do next.

"Your father's here," Joelle said from the doorway to Bryce's office. "Do you want me to send him in or tell him you're busy?"

Peter Delaney visited the office when he wanted Bryce to act as a go-between with his mother. The two only spoke when attending the same social event, where they limited their exchanges to polite platitudes. Bryce had assumed the mediator role as a child, but dealing with one of his parents' endless battles when he felt so broken up inside didn't appeal to him in the slightest.

"Did he say why he wants to see me?" Bryce asked.

"Only that it was important," Joelle said.

He stared at the code on his monitor. He'd thrown himself into work for over a week now, but the long hours hadn't made him feel any better over what had happened with Dani. If anything, work made him feel worse. They'd met through the Web site. Every time he logged on, he thought about her.

Dani would never admit she needed anything, not even love, if that meant she had to rely on someone except herself. She hadn't wanted his help. She hadn't wanted him. And there wasn't a damn thing he could do about it. Not unless he wanted to be accused of trying to "control."

"Boss?" Joelle asked.

Maybe talking with his father would take his mind off her. Something had to. Bryce saved and closed the file. "Send him in."

A minute later, his father sauntered in, checking out Joelle's backside as she walked away. "How's it going, son?"

"Fine."

Peter sat. He studied the stacks of papers on the desk, grimaced and looked at Bryce. "Your mother's worried about you."

"Caitlin called you."

"No, Maeve called me herself."

Bryce straightened.

"That's why I'm here," Peter admitted. "She's very concerned about you, Bryce. You haven't returned any of her phone calls."

Bryce wasn't ready to tell his family he was no longer dating Dani. He hadn't wanted the questions or the company. "It's been a hectic week."

"You haven't been home. Your mother and I stopped by your house last night."

"You and Mother together at my place. I hope I still have a house to go home to."

Peter frowned. "We may not be the best parents, but we're adult enough to put aside our differences for our children's sake."

A bitter guilt coated Bryce's mouth. Even he could see his father was here trying to help. "Sorry. Rough week."

"Were you with Dani last night?"

"No, I slept here at the office," Bryce admitted. "I've been putting in more hours lately."

Not that he'd been getting anything done.

The lines on his father's face relaxed. "Your mother will be relieved."

"You seem relieved, too."

"We like Dani, but you haven't been together long. Your mother is worried you might be rushing into something. She thinks you might be thinking about following in Edward's footsteps and eloping to Las Vegas."

Bryce winced. "Not going to happen."

"But if things do get more serious, you have to start thinking about a prenup."

He shook his head. "I don't have to worry about that."

Not now.

"One of these days, you will," Peter counseled. "You have so much to lose, including half of your share of this company."

"I—"

"Hear me out, Bryce," Peter said. "You said Dani was a smart woman."

"She is."

"Her brains match her body."

"They do."

"Your mother is like that." Peter's eyes narrowed. "Women like your mother will take you for everything you've got."

"Dani's not like my mother."

Peter raised a brow. "How do you know?"

"I trust her." And he did, Bryce realized in spite of everything. "Dani wants to be independent. She won't take anything from me."

*Not even my heart.*

Peter stood. "Just remember, son, a man has every right to protect himself."

*You don't want to protect. You want to control.*

Dani had been right about his trying to control things with her, but he hadn't known the reason until now.

Being in control was the way Bryce protected himself.

The realization brought a rush of shame and a flash of clarity.

But controlling things hadn't worked. He'd lost what mattered most.

Dani.

Peter walked toward the door. "Call your mother."

"I will," Bryce said. "Thanks for coming by."

His father smiled. "Catch you later, son."

Bryce dialed Dani's cell number. One ring, two rings. The line connected. Every one of his muscles tensed.

"I'm sorry," an automated voice said. "This wireless number is no longer in service."

He grabbed his keys, told Joelle to cancel all his

appointments for the day and drove to Dani's apartment. He parked illegally, not caring if he got a ticket or was towed.

He'd known what she'd needed, but done the exact opposite. Sure he'd thought about her, but he'd also been thinking about himself. Just like…her father.

Bryce took the stairs three at a time. He knocked on Dani's door.

Something clicked. The knob turned.

He breathed a sigh of relief.

The door opened.

"What do you want?" asked a man dressed in a pirate costume complete with eye patch and a real parrot on his shoulder.

Bryce's heart fell. "I was looking for the woman who used to live here."

"She's gone."

"Gone," the parrot mimicked. "Long gone."

"Do you know where she went?"

"Nope, but if you find her tell her thanks for cleaning this place so well."

Bryce walked back to his car, trying to figure out what to do next. He had never let anything stand between him and what he wanted and he'd never wanted anything, he'd never needed anyone, as much as he wanted and needed Dani.

Bryce was going to make things right. He would make things work. Somehow.

But first he had to find her.

Dani speared a clump with a pitchfork. She hadn't mucked stalls in over a year and already the muscles in her arms and shoulders ached. Good thing she'd remembered gloves or she'd have blisters on her hands.

Her pitchfork scraped the wheelbarrow.

The smell of horse and hay reminded her of the day at the stable with Bryce. Her mind burned with the memory.

Of her riding.

Of the sexy smile on Bryce's face as he'd watched her.

Of the passionate kiss they'd shared.

*Stop thinking about him.* Dani squeezed her eyes closed, trying to force the images from her mind.

It was over. She opened her eyes. Over.

She stabbed another clump.

The horse from the next stall neighed.

Her boots crunched beneath the mixture of straw and shavings.

"Just be patient, Penny," Dani said to the pretty little chestnut mare. "Your stall is next."

The horse snorted.

"I know how you feel." She leaned against the

pitchfork handle and rolled her shoulders. "It's not easy being patient."

But Dani finally had a plan in place. She wiped her sweaty forehead with her forearm. She'd spent the last three days e-mailing her résumés to more companies. This morning, she'd even had a phone interview for a position in Raleigh, North Carolina. That was on the other side of the country, but nothing was stopping her from taking a job anywhere in the world. No one cared where she ended up except her mom, and she only wanted Dani to be happy wherever that might be.

She sifted through the clumps. The physical work felt good, satisfying.

"I wondered whether you'd be wearing a bandana," a much too familiar voice said.

As Dani clutched the pitchfork handle, she pivoted toward the doorway.

Bryce stood at the entrance to the stall. Her stomach fell to the tips of her paddock boots. He stared at her as if he were seeing her for the first time. And liked what he saw. Dani ground her boot against the floor.

She stole another glance his way. Sweat beaded on his forehead as if he were nervous about something. Not so calm and collected today. That surprised her.

He also looked out of place in his dress pants and

Oxford shirt with the sleeves rolled up and the top button undone at his neck.

Out of place, but handsome as ever. Not that she cared what he looked like, Dani reminded herself.

"How did you find me?" she asked.

"Once I figured out you'd moved, I found your two friends' user names on a chat log I had. Unfortunately for me, Kangagirl and Englishcrumpet weren't about to give you up until I'd convinced them I had your best interests in mind. But they were easier to convince than your mother."

Dani's mouth dropped open. She closed it. "My mother?"

Bryce nodded. "I spent the last hour talking to her."

"Whatever you said must have worked."

Another nod.

"You went to a lot of trouble to find me." She eyed him warily. "Why?"

"I wanted to see you."

She noticed the dirt smudges on the sides of his fine leather shoes. "All that just to see me."

"And to explain."

"Go ahead then." Dani wanted to feel indifferent and kept her voice steady, but inside she trembled. Heaven help her, she wanted to hear what he had to say. "I'm listening."

"Before I say anything—" he strode across the stall toward her "—I need to do this first."

"Do—"

Bryce pressed his lips firmly against hers, taking what he wanted and giving back what Dani so desperately needed. His warm, wet kiss filled her up, and she wanted more. She kissed him back with an eagerness of her own. As he pulled her closer, she wrapped her arms around him. The pitchfork crashed to the floor of the stall.

Bryce pulled back, his gaze never leaving hers.

Oh, my. Oh, no. Dani wiped her mouth with the back of her gloved hand, afraid what her response to his kiss might have told him. She raised her chin. "Something else you think I need?"

"Something I needed." His eyes gleamed. Anger or something else, she couldn't tell. "I need you, Dani."

Her breath caught in her throat. She hadn't been expecting that.

"I'm sorry for not trusting you to handle James on your own," he said, his tone genuine and his voice strong. "I thought all this time I only wanted to protect the people I care about, but you're right. I've only been trying to control things. That's my way of protecting myself. My heart."

The sincerity of his words, the honesty in his eyes, brought tears to her eyes. Deep inside, a sliver of hope sparked.

"I've been doing that ever since my parents'

divorce to keep from getting hurt, but I didn't realize what I was doing until you pointed it out."

"I appreciate you coming all this way to say that." She cleared her dry throat. "It means…a lot."

"You mean a lot to me," Bryce continued. "You said I was like your father, but I'm not him. I'm here. I'm not going anywhere. Even if you push me away, I will still love you."

His words reverberated through her. The oxygen seemed to evaporate from the air. She might as well be twenty feet underwater, the way she struggled to breathe.

Bryce loved her.

"I've needed to hear you say that," she said. "Even though you said they were just words."

"Words are important, and I can say them as many times as you want."

"Thanks, but saying the words doesn't change things." Dani wanted to ignore the truth, but couldn't. "You like being in control, Bryce. You like protecting people. That's who you are, and I'm afraid I'll lose myself, the way my mother did with my father, if I'm with you."

"I know being independent is important to you, but I love you. I have to be able to protect you. You're strong enough, though, to stand up to me and let me know when you need help or when you don't. And I'm smart enough to learn." He raised her chin with his fingertip. "You're not your mother. You've never been her."

A million thoughts ran through Dani's mind. But only one came to the forefront, as clear as the Golden Gate Bridge on a sunny day.

Bryce.

"You're right. I'm not." She stared up at him. "But I never wanted to be hurt again, the way my father hurt me. I figured if I didn't rely on anyone, it couldn't happen again."

"I never wanted to hurt you, Dani."

"I see that now." Her cheeks warmed. "And I never meant to hurt you, either."

"We've both been protecting ourselves."

She nodded. "I'm sorry, Bryce. I've been using anything I could—your background and your money—the same way I used my baggy clothes, to keep you at a distance. Just like a heroine from a Jane Austen novel."

"That's okay." He smiled. "So long as I don't lose you to the Colonel."

"Don't worry about him." Dani removed her gloves and placed her hand on Bryce's chest. His heart beat beneath her palm. "You might be a Web tycoon, but you're also a caring man who reaches out to others, whether it's me, your family or Blinddatebrides.com users looking for love. You're definitely Colonel Brandon material."

"Even without a uniform?"

Warmth flowed through her veins. She nodded. "You, Bryce Delaney, are my Colonel Brandon."

Bryce's smile widened. "From the moment you entered my life, I needed you. I'll always be here for you. I love you, Dani Bennett."

"Oh, Bryce." Joy overflowed from her heart. "I love you, too."

He pulled her into his arms and kissed her. A kiss of hope. A kiss of promise.

"You decide what you want to do yourself and what you don't. I'll support you either way." He tightened his arms around her. "Together we can make our dreams come true."

She gazed up at him. "That sounds wonderful, but it's not as simple as that."

"No?"

"For this to work and to last, we have to trust each other. Take care of me, but let me take care of you, too. I'll tell you what I'm thinking and feeling and you have to do the same."

"I'm not used to being taken care of, but I want this to work and to last. I'm willing to try," he said.

"You said you're smart enough to learn."

"That I did," Bryce admitted. "Have no worries, Miss Bennett, I am and I will."

Tingles exploded inside of her. "So we're back together, dating again."

"I think we've skipped right on over to serious relationship."

"Fine with me."

"Me, too." He brushed his lips across the top of her head. "Now we just have to figure out what comes next."

"That's easy," she said without any hesitation. "We head back to San Francisco."

"You're sure about that?"

She nodded. "I finally know where home is."

Bryce kissed her gently on the lips. A strange expression crossed his face. "This isn't how I planned things, but hang on."

Confused, Dani watched him run out of the stall and return with a large box that he placed on the ground. "What…?"

He dropped to his knee.

"You'll ruin your pants," she said.

"I can buy a new pair."

He held on to her hand.

A mixture of anticipation and nerves made her hold her breath. She was too stunned to believe, too hopeful to doubt.

He stared up into her eyes as if she were the earth and heaven to him. "Being without you has only made it clearer that I want to be with you always. I don't want you to ever question what I mean by us being in a relationship. Will you marry me, Dani Bennett?"

Her heart soared, but her brain dragged her back to the ground. Was marriage to Bryce what she wanted?

Her heart screamed the answer. It was time to move forward with this man who loved her, a man she loved back.

"Yes." Dani laughed. "Of course I'll marry you. I love you, Bryce."

"I love you."

He stood and sealed the proposal with a kiss.

"Ever since I was a little girl, I never felt like I belonged anywhere. But when I'm with you, I do." Dani smiled up at him through tears of happiness. "I feel safe, secure and loved. Nothing else matters as long as we're together."

"I don't have an engagement ring for you, but I do have these." He removed the top from the box and pulled out a pair of new paddock boots. "I bought these for you after we went to look at the horse. I figured you could use an extra pair. One to wear when you're hanging around the stable and another pair for when you ride."

Dani touched the shiny leather. "These are more practical than any ring."

"You're still getting a ring. I want to put a big one on your finger. Not practical, but you deserve it. And I want the world to know that you're with me."

"Do you plan to carry me off like some caveman, too?" she teased.

He grunted. "If that's what it takes."

Things couldn't get any better. Dani's entire body seemed to be smiling.

"Can I put the boots on you?" he asked.

She stilled. "Just like Cinderella."

"Well, if the shoe fits…" Bryce reached for her left foot. "But they aren't exactly glass slippers."

Dani's heart sang. "They're better."

She leaned against a wall of the stable while he pulled off the old boots and put on the new ones. These were what she wanted, what she needed. Just like him. Bryce really did know her.

This was like a fairy tale come true, but with no fairy godmother required.

"How do they feel?" Bryce asked when he'd finished.

The love in his voice brought a sigh to her lips. She straightened, leaned back on her heels and wiggled her toes. "A perfect fit."

"Perfect fit, huh?"

She nodded. "Just like us."

"I could have told you that."

"Your compatibility program did."

He smiled. "I don't need a computer algorithm to tell me what my heart's known all along."

Dani saw not only her dreams coming, but a lifetime of love in his eyes. "What's that?"

"The two of us are perfect for each other."

# EPILOGUE

To: "Englishcrumpet" <englishcrumpet@blind-datebrides.com>
"Kangagirl" <kangagirl@blinddatebrides.com>
From: "Sanfrandani" <sanfrandani@blinddate-brides.com>
Subject: Let's schedule a chat!
I have so much to tell you, but the biggest news is…

I'm engaged! Can you believe it???

We considered eloping for about thirty seconds, but know a long engagement makes smarter sense. Plus then maybe you both can come!

Bryce said you two told him where to find me. Thank you so much! You are the best friends ever!!! xoxox

Love,

Dani

P.S. Bryce reactivated my Blinddatebrides.com account.

P.P.S. Do you think six bridesmaids would be too many? My three sisters, Bryce's and the two of you!!!

* * * * *

*Celebrate 60 years of pure reading pleasure
with Harlequin®!*

*Harlequin Presents® is proud to introduce its
gripping new miniseries,*
**THE ROYAL HOUSE OF KAREDES.**
*An exquisite coronation diamond, split as a
symbol of a warring royal family's feud, is
missing! But whoever reunites the diamond halves
will rule all....*

*Welcome to eight brand-new titles that unfold to
reveal the stories of kings and queens, princes
and princesses torn apart by pride and power, but
finally reunited by love.*

*Step into the world of Karedes with*
*BILLIONAIRE PRINCE, PREGNANT MISTRESS*
*Available July 2009
from Harlequin Presents®.*

ALEXANDROS KAREDES, SNOW DUSTING the shoulders of his leather jacket and glittering like jewels in his dark hair, stood at the door. Maria felt the blood drain from her head.

"Good evening, Ms. Santos."

His voice was as she remembered it. Deep. Husky. Perfect English, but with the faintest hint of a Greek accent. And cold, as cold as it had been that awful morning she would never forget, when he'd accused her of horrible things, called her terrible names....

"Aren't you going to ask me in?"

She fought for composure. Last time they'd faced each other, they'd been on his turf. Now they were on hers. She was in command here, and that meant everything.

"There's a sign on the door downstairs," she said, her tone every bit as frigid as his. "It says, 'No soliciting or vagrants.'"

His lips drew back in a wolfish grin. "Very amusing."

"What do you want, Prince Alexandros?"

A tight smile eased across his mouth and it killed her that even now, knowing he was a vicious, arrogant man, she couldn't help but notice what a handsome mouth it was. Chiseled. Generous. Beautiful, like the rest of him, which made him living proof that beauty could, indeed, be only skin deep.

"Such formality, Maria. You were hardly so proper the last time we were together."

She knew his choice of words was deliberate. She felt her face heat; she couldn't help that but she damned well didn't have to let him lure her into a verbal sparring match.

"I'll ask you once more, your highness. What do you want?"

"Ask me in and I'll tell you."

"I have no intention of asking you in. Tell me why you're here or don't. It's your choice, just as it will be my choice to shut the door in your face."

He laughed. It infuriated her but she could hardly blame him. He was tall—six two, six three—and though he stood with one shoulder leaning against the door frame, hands tucked casually into the pockets of the jacket, his pose was deceptive. He was strong, with the leanly muscled body of a well-trained athlete.

She remembered his body with painful clarity. The feel of him under her hands. The power of him moving over her. The taste of him on her tongue.

Suddenly, he straightened, his laughter gone. "I have not come this distance to stand in your doorway," he said coldly, "and I am not going to leave until I am ready to do so. I suggest you stand aside and stop behaving like a petulant child."

A petulant child? Was that what he thought? This man who had spent hours making love to her and had then accused her of—of trading her body for profit?

Except it had not been love, it had been sex. And the sooner she got rid of him, the better.

She let go of the doorknob and stepped aside. "You have five minutes."

He strolled past her, bringing cold air and the scent of the night with him. She swung toward him, arms folded. He reached past her, pushed the door closed, then folded his arms, too. She wanted to open the door again but she'd be damned if she was going to get into a who's-in-charge-here argument with him. She was in charge, and he would surely see a tussle over the ground rules as a sign of weakness.

Instead, she looked past him at the big clock above her work table.

"Ten seconds gone," she said briskly. "You're wasting time, your highness."

"What I have to say will take longer than five minutes."

"Then you'll just have to learn to economize. More than five minutes, I'll call the police."

Instantly, his hand was wrapped around her wrist. He tugged her toward him, his dark-chocolate eyes almost black with anger.

"You do that and I'll tell every tabloid shark I can contact about how Maria Santos tried to buy a five-hundred-thousand-dollar commission by seducing a prince." He smiled thinly. "They'll lap it up."

\* \* \* \* \*

*What will it take for this billionaire prince*
*to realize he's falling in love*
*with his mistress…?*
*Look for*
*BILLIONAIRE PRINCE, PREGNANT MISTRESS*
*by Sandra Marton*
*Available July 2009*
*from Harlequin Presents®.*